BEGIN *Again*

TAMSYN BESTER

BEGIN AGAIN

Edited by Emma Mack, Tink's Typos
Cover Design © by Sommer Stein, Perfect Pear Creative Covers
PHOTO COPYRIGHT © Toski Covey, Toski Covey Photography - Custom Design
Formatting by Max Effect Author Services

Acknowledgements

Firstly, I'd like to thank my parents, my family and my friends for their continued support. It means the world to me!

Then to my amazing team of Beta readers who always made time to read the bits & pieces of this book I sent! Thank you goes to Shanora Williams, Michelle Davis Grad, Emma Mack, Susan Davis Provorse, Ullanda Artis, and Sirenda McNece – can't thank you ladies enough!! To Christine Stanley at This Redhead Loves Books, who is the genius responsible for my PR, it has been so much fun getting to know you! Your support is greatly appreciated, as is all your hard work ♥

Then, a very special thanks goes out to Michelle Davis Grad and Emma Mack! Michelle a.k.a Mamma, you have been with me from the beginning, ever since Beneath Your Beautiful popped into my head, and I am so grateful for everything you've done to help me! Love your face! Then Emma, I'm not sure if this book would be finished if it weren't for all our Skype sessions! THANK YOU ♥

I'd also like to thank Toski Covey at Toski Covey Photography – Custom Design, and Sommer Stein at Perfect Pear Creative for another amazing cover! To my cover models, Mariah Jane and D.J Adkins – you are my perfect Demi and Brody, THANK YOU ♥

And finally, to my amazing readers! Without you I wouldn't be living this dream ♥ THANK YOU ♥

A Note From The Author

Begin Again has by far been my greatest challenge and it has been an incredibly tiring journey to write this story, both mentally and emotionally. I wrote it at a very difficult time in my life when I was experiencing so many changes.

Demi and Brody's story was not an easy feat but I pushed through because my readers wanted their story. I hope it isn't a disappointment, and that each and very reader who asked for, or more like demanded, I write this will fall in love with these characters.

No one can really explain what it takes to sit down and write a book - by the end you're left exhausted, and stripped bare, and when you send it out into the world, you hope and pray that someone will love it as much as you do. I am very proud of this story and I feel I that Demi and Brody deserved having their book written.

Finally, I would like to thank the readers who demanded this story be written - I hope you love the hell out of it!

All my love,

Tamsyn

chapter one

1 Year Ago

DEMI

I collapsed on Brody's chest, his heart racing right alongside mine. We were exhausted but it had been worth getting to that point. The sheets were gathered around my waist, covering us from my hips down, and the pillows were strewn across the room. The last streaks of sunlight shone across his muscular stomach, making him look like a God, basked in eternal sunlight. I looked up, resting my chin between his pectoral muscles, and found his half-lidded gaze fixed on me.

His dirty blonde hair was a mess, sticking up in every direction. He looked so damn sexy that way. I smiled and he wiped my hair from my sweaty forehead. "What?" I asked with a light, breathless giggle. Brody's mouth tipped up into a lazy grin that made my insides do flip-flops. Not that it took much from him to solicit that response, or any response for that matter, from my body. He knew what got me going and that grin just happened to be one of those things.

"That was…incredible," he murmured. "That thing you did with your hips was new." I blushed and bit my lip. "I might have to do it again when you're misbehavin'."

"I might let you," he sighed, looking content. "You look gorgeous like this." His voice had that rich timber to it that made women want to rip off their own underwear and throw it at him. It made my insides quiver and I tried hard not to squeeze my thighs together in anticipation. He was still buried in deep and if I had to squeeze anything he'd be ready to go again. I needed rest so there was no need for me to stir the beast a fourth time.

I scrunched my nose. "I look gorgeous sweaty and out of breath?"

He chuckled and the vibrations bounced between us before crash landing at the spot where we were still connected. "Especially when you're sweaty and out of breath."

I slapped his chest playfully and he caught my wrist. "You just like getting me this way," I said. "You're a caveman."

His lips brushed my pulse and my breath stuttered. I felt him stir between my legs and the sensations made me squirm.

"Only with you, baby," he whispered. He licked his lips and without warning sat upright. His arms wrapped around my back and he shifted me forward so that we stayed joined. I felt him harden.

"Again?" I asked. I shouldn't have been surprised though. Brody had more stamina than a raging Bull during mating season. He knew how to take pleasure from my body and he knew how to give it. The man was a talent in the sack and he knew it. He was also all mine.

Brody watched me intently, his brown eyes searching my face. Suddenly I wondered if he'd somehow figured out my secret. But how? I'd only found out earlier today and had every intention of telling him my news. Well, our news. But that was before he attacked me and took me to bed. Not that I was complaining. I liked where we were, the way our bodies were positioned as if they were made for the other.

Brody's voice came quietly, but I had no trouble hearing him. "I need to tell you something."

I swallowed hard. Oh God, I thought. He knows. He's going to leave me.

"O-okay," I stuttered, blood rushing to my ears.

"I got a call today." Oh crap, someone from the doctor's office called him and told him I'm – "I got a job offer in Chicago."

I started apologizing before what he said registered. "I'm so sorry Brody, I should've – wait, what? You got a call from Chicago?"

My body sagged. At least now I would be the one to tell him, instead of having to hear from a nurse at the hospital.

"The C.E.O of Johnson Waterman called me. A job opened up in their agency and they're offering it to me."

Johnson Waterman was one of the biggest and most successful sports recruitment agencies in the United States. Brody had been waiting for this opportunity since graduating two years before and now that it was in front of him, I had no idea how to respond. Of course my nerves had everything to do with what I had to tell him since it could very well change everything, not only for him, but for both of us together.

"That's amazing, Brody," I said with a half smile. The look in his brown eyes told me he wasn't buying it. I never did have a good poker face. Then again, neither did Brody. Everything started to click into place and I realized that Brody had used sex to butter me up for this. That's why he had been so impatient when I got home.

He opened his mouth to speak but I beat him to it. "Is that why you were so eager to get me into bed?" My half-smile faltered when he hesitated and looked down. I tried to pull away but he wouldn't have it and tightened his grip.

"Will you listen to me, please?" he pleaded softly. He was patronizing me and I hated it. It was supposed to be a good day for us but I couldn't help but feel my excitement fade. I should've told him, I chastise myself internally. Then maybe we'd be having an entirely different conversation.

"This is a big opportunity for me," he started, "for us. Think about the life we can have in Chicago. Just you and me." I wanted to add and our baby but it wasn't exactly how I had envisioned telling him I was pregnant. Surprise.

I stared at him, unable to reconcile the man in front of me with the man whose baby I was carrying. I wanted a family with Brody more than anything, but I wanted to stay here in Breckinridge.

"I can't leave now, Brody. Graduation is less than a month away and I've already accepted the job at Breckinridge Elementary next year."

"Then you come to Chicago after Graduation and we can find you a job at a school there. Or even better, you don't have to work."

I shook my head. "No." I shoved at his chest and his grip finally loosened enough for me to get off his lap. I winced, feeling a little a sensitive between my legs, and grabbed a sheet to wrap myself in. Brody was sitting buck ass naked in the middle of my King-size bed and I hardly noticed. I was too preoccupied with how he'd planned out our entire lives without talking to me about it.

"I don't understand what the big deal is, Demetria. This has been my dream and - "

"Don't you dare," I interrupted, pointing my finger at him from across the room. "You know how I feel about leaving here and still, you make this big decision for both of us without talking to me about it first."

Brody climbed off the bed and slipped his jeans on, not bothering to button them up.

"I'm talking to you about it now aren't I?"

I snorted. "Yes, after we had sex three times and after you'd already made the decision without me. How does that seem fair?"

Brody threw his arms up, clearly as exasperated with me as I was with him. "Fair? You want to talk about fair? What about the fact that I'm miserable here, but I suck it up to make you happy? What about my dreams huh? Do you think I want to be stuck here for the rest of my life?"

I froze and my eyes widened. His words hit me like a bulldozer and I struggled to inhale oxygen into my lungs. Brody saw the shock on my face and stepped closer but I put my hand up to stop him. I hugged the sheet closer to me, as if it would somehow make the hurt pounding in my chest go away.

"I didn't mean it like that," he said loudly. My eyes traveled over his face, taking in the roguish features that had become so familiar to me. He might've been all man now, but in his eyes I saw the little boy I'd loved all my life.

"You're not happy with me." It was a statement, rather than a question.

"That's not what - "

"When do you leave?"

He sighed and rubbed his face before resting his hands on his hips. "I fly out tomorrow to meet with the C.E.O."

"Tomorrow?" I almost yell. My hand instinctively goes to my flat belly but Brody doesn't notice.

"It all happened so quickly," he retorts quickly. "What was I supposed to do? Turn down my dream job?"

"Talk to me first!" I screamed. "This doesn't only change your life, Brody! It changes mine too!"

"I get that, Demetria, I do! That's why I said you can come to Chicago when you've graduated and we can be together."

I wiped my face, furious that I was crying. I never cried. It wasn't part of who I was. I simply picked myself up and moved on, like I had always done. But now my hormones were all over the place and there was no stopping that or the tears running down my face.

"So that's it then? You're going and I'm supposed to follow you when I'm done with school?"

"Fuck, Demi, I want to build a life for us, why can't you understand that?"

"What's wrong with the life we have here?" I asked. I hiccupped and fought the bile clawing its way up my throat.

Brody hung his head and shook it. "It's not the life I want for us."

"Stop doing that, stop saying 'for us'. I like my life here, and what we have is enough - "

"Not for me," Brody snapped, cutting me off. "I need more, Demi."

I reared back as if he'd slapped me and sucked in a sharp breath. I took a step back and pulled myself together long enough to say what I needed to.

"Obviously you've made up your mind," I swallowed, willing the words to come out before the vomit did, "and I've made up mine."

"You're coming with me?" Brody sounded hopeful. I hated myself for giving him that hope, but I wasn't only thinking about myself. Brody and I clearly wanted different things and I'd spent too many years not putting myself first.

"No," I whispered hoarsely, shaking my head. "My home is here."

I turned around and walked into the bathroom, shutting the door behind me.

"Demi," Brody called me through the door. "Please, baby."

I ignored the plea in his voice and cupped my mouth to muffle the sobs wracking from my body. I couldn't bring myself to speak to him. I was afraid one look into his eyes would weaken my resolve and I'd end up agreeing to go with him. I couldn't risk that. After a while it got quiet and I was sure Brody had left, but when I opened the door he was perched on the edge of the bed with elbows on his knees and his head in his hands. He looked up and for a brief moment I considered what he was asking me to do. I walked to my dresser and instead of pulling out one of Brody's shirts, I took out my lime green sleep shorts and matching tank top. I got dressed, aware that Brody's eyes never left my body, and left the room. I sat on the sofa and tucked my feet under my butt. It wasn't long before I heard Brody's feet echo down the hallway and when he joined me I still couldn't look at him. It was all too much. He'd made his choice without me, assuming that I'd pack up my life and go after him. He was one of few people who understood why my independence was important to me and now it felt like he was one of the first to take it away. The worst part was I still had to tell him about the baby, only I worried that if he knew, he'd stay out of obligation. How could I have kept him here if he was so desperate to leave?

"I didn't mean to upset you." Brody spoke softly and I knew he meant to comfort me, sooth me, but all I felt was cold. My greatest fear had always been losing him, but now it was losing myself.

"You're going to ask me to make a choice," I said. My voice trembled. "And I won't pick you. Chicago is your dream, not mine, and I would never ask you to give up that dream for me. But you're asking me to give up my d-dream," I took a breath and calmed my emotions as best as I could, " and I c-can't d-do that."

"What can I do to change your mind? What can I say to get you to come with me?"

I looked down, noting how my tears dropped into my hands, and replied, "You can't." When I looked back up his expression was unreadable and I wished mine were too. I was a mess and Brody looked too composed, too put together.

"So what now?" he asked. I wanted nothing more than to crawl into his lap and hold him, feel his heart beat steady against my palm. The feeling that it was all slipping away hung heavy in the air.

"I don't know," I replied softly. I got up and stood between Brody's legs, drinking him in one last time. I cupped his face with my hands and bent down to kiss him for what felt like the last time. His lips were warm and slightly rough, the perfect opposite to my soft and salty.

"I love you," I whispered. "Always."

I walked away then, leaving him there alone, and when I woke up a few hours later, he was gone. He'd packed a bag and left, without saying goodbye. I rested my hand over my non-existent bump and cried. "Looks like it's just you and me now kid."

chapter two

Present Day

Demi

The early morning sun seeped through my half-open curtains and warmed my cheeks. I felt movement next to my bed, and the sounds of little whimpers. I rolled over, and cracked an eye open, peering down. Two chocolate brown eyes and a wet nose greeted me.

"G'morning Coco," I greeted. I stretched and wrapped my hands around my puppy's little brown body, lifting her onto the bed. Her tail wagged furiously, and her tongue licked my face, returning my hello with one of her own.

"Are you hungry?" I cooed, giggling from her sweet, wet kisses. This was our morning ritual, and it always made me smile. I slipped a pair of thin sleep shorts on over my panties, and padded down the hallway to my kitchen, my brown

Labrador hot on my heels. I took her outside to do her business and as soon as I placed her bowl of puppy food on the hardwood floor, Coco started yapping excitedly. I rubbed her ears before putting a fresh K-cup in my Keurig and noted that the clock on the wall read nine a.m. I had an hour before I had to be at Huntley and Grayson's house for Saturday lunch. Another weekly ritual I'd become fond of in the last few months. As I sat down on the deck overlooking my small, neatly kept garden, my body sighed in appreciation for the beautiful morning sunshine, clean air and rich aroma of my coffee. For the first time in what seemed like forever, I felt better, and a little more like myself. It's been a year, and not a day passed when I didn't think about Brody, and what I'd lost, but instead of the crippling pain I usually I felt when I thought about him, it became a dull ache that I was able to cover with temporary band aids. After I graduated, I got a job as a second grade elementary school teacher at Breckinridge elementary. My parents bought me a small, but spacious, cottage-style house as a graduation present, and as always, they thought it made up for the absence throughout most of my life. I wasn't prepared to turn it down, no matter how angry I was that they were once again absent for one of the biggest days of my life. Brody and I lived in the apartment I used to share with Huntley, after she moved in with Grayson, and once I graduated I moved into my house. For the most part we were happy, until Brody made a choice that changed everything for us.

Coco scratched at my leg, interrupting my wayward thoughts, and I grinned down at her. I scratched her belly, finished my coffee, and got dressed before grabbing my purse and heading out the door.

****

I pulled into huntley and Grayson's driveway and stopped in front of their double garage. Their house was stunning on the outside, and everything I could imagine Huntley wanting – white picket fence, blue shutters, wraparound porch. As soon as I walked in through the front door Hunter came barreling down the hallway, and flung himself into my body, nearly knocking me off my feet.

"Mimi!" he yelled excitedly. I bent down and allowed him to wrap his arms around my neck. He squeezed tight, and whispered, "I missed you," in my ear so that only I could hear.

I squeezed him back, and pulled away to look at his handsome little face. "Hey booger. I missed you too."

He grinned a wide, toothy grin, and my heart filled with love for my Godson. I stood up, took his hand in mine and walked into the kitchen. Grayson's mother, May, was standing in front of the stove, while Huntley's aunt, Emma, was filling glasses with what I assumed was her sweet tea. Huntley was leaning against the counter, laughing at something her aunt said.

"Hey Dem," Huntley greeted. She hugged me, and I returned it.

"Hey girl," I replied. Huntley's eyes searched mine, and it was a look I'd become familiar with months ago. It was probing. She was trying to gauge how I was feeling. If it were anyone else my defenses would've shot right up. But she was my best friend, and she understood how hard the last year had been for me.

"You seem better today," she remarked. "I'm glad to see that smile again. I missed it."

I gave her hand a squeeze, and replied, "I'm good."

Huntley's eyes were bright with understanding, and I knew she was glad that I was feeling more like the old me. After I greeted May, and Emma, Huntley and I took a seat at the island in the middle of the kitchen. Huntley looked a little worried, and opened and closed her mouth a few times before talking.

"I need to tell you something," she said. Her gaze dropped momentarily, and then lifted back to mine. My heart sank, because I knew what she wanted to tell me.

"I know he's coming tomorrow," I said, beating her to the punch. She was going to tell me Brody would be arriving tomorrow, which I already knew. Huntley and Grayson's wedding was only a week away, and since Brody and I were both part of the wedding party, I figured he'd want to be here for everything that was planned for the week ahead. I was Huntleys' Maid of Honor, but luckily Jeff was Grayson's' best man, which meant he'd be my date.

Huntley's shoulders dropped, and she sighed in relief. "Who told you?"

"Jeff," I replied, fighting the urge to smile at the sound of his name.

Huntleys' mouth tipped into a knowing smirk. "He's been calling you hasn't he," she observed.

I nodded. "Yeah. Almost every night." I felt a knot form in my stomach at the admission, and I knew it was guilt.

"You have nothing to feel bad about," Huntley said, reading my thoughts. "He makes you feel like you again, and there's nothing wrong with that."

"We're just friends," I sighed, knowing that it's a partial lie. Huntley's brows rose and I could tell she didn't believe me. She knew me better than that. Huntley took my hands, and held them, giving me a sympathetic gaze. "You have no reason at all to feel guilty. I know Jeff helped you get through a lot, and if I'm being honest, I'm glad he did. I know you care about him, Dem, and he cares about you too." Jeff was another member of the Carter family that I grew up with, so we'd been friends since we were kids. But he'd become something more to me. I needed someone to hold me up when everything around me, and inside me, was falling apart and Jeff was there. Somewhere along the way something happened and I'd started seeing him a little differently. Even so, I never acted on those feelings because at the time I was emotionally unavailable and he knew that, but didn't seem to mind.

"I know," I replied. I tried not to think about everything too much and on most days, like today, I actually got it right. It wasn't always easy for me to talk about, even to Huntley, but I understood how important it was to do what I had to in order to move forward, and put myself back together. It helped that Huntley and I worked at the same school. I'd spent many lunch breaks in her counselors' office talking it out, crying if needed. Of course, that was after I took a short leave of absence *after* everything that happened when Brody left. The school insisted I take more time after everything I'd been through, but I reached a point where being at home drove me crazy and I grew tired of the mind-numbing pills that made me feel nothing for far too long. I was stronger than that and I only realized that when I was the only person who could pull me out of the hole I had fallen into. Sure, I had Huntley and Grayson to help me, Jeff too. In fact, I had the whole Carter family, and the Morgan family, taking care of me. But I needed to draw on my own strength to pull myself through my grief. After a while, the sunshine started coming through the darkness again and I reveled in it when those moments came. Eventually, I started feeling okay again. I accepted that I could never be who I used to be, especially after what I had lost, but I found a new determination. I wasn't ready to lose myself. So I fought and I fought hard. All that fire inside me led me to today, to feeling more like myself than I had in months.

"There you girls are."

I looked up just as Grayson walked in. I stood up and he

pulled me into his body for a bear hug. He'd become a little bigger since he graduated. Working at the new Sports Rehabilitation center kept him fit and he looked good.

"Hey Gray," I sighed, hugging him around his waist.

"Good to see you, Demi," he said, smiling at me. He let me go and lifted Huntley off her chair before taking her place and depositing her in his lap. "What's this I hear about my brother?" he asked, looking between Huntley and me curiously.

I looked down and felt my cheeks heat.

"Now that's a sight for sore eyes," Grayson mumbled. I looked up to find him and Huntley grinning at me like fools.

"What?" I asked.

"You're blushing," Grayson remarked. "I didn't know if we'd ever see that again."

I knew what he meant. Grayson was Brody's best friend, but he was one of mine too and he cared about me. I wasn't sure how things were between him and Brody now but I knew their relationship had been strained for a while after he left. Grayson was pissed that Brody left, and he wanted me to tell him about what happened to me, but I just couldn't. I wasn't ready then and the one time I tried it blew up in my face. Luckily, I had Jeff to help me get through yet another one of life's disappointments.

"Your brother has been good to me, Gray."

"I know. We're just glad to have you smiling again. I know Hunter has missed you too."

I smiled thinking about my adorable Godson. I missed him too, even though I'd seen him regularly. He often went with Huntley to school on the days she worked and during lunch I'd steal him for a while. He was always so happy, and it was impossible to dwell on life's shortcomings with him around. Huntley and Grayson were both worried that being around Hunter would be difficult for me, but it was actually quite the opposite. Now that it was summer vacation and Huntley and I were on a break, I could see him more often.

As if knowing we were talking about him, Hunter came sauntering into the kitchen, swinging his arms and shaking his little hips. For a two year old, he sure had attitude.

"Hey bud." Grayson smiled proudly at his son. He was the perfect mixture of Huntley and Grayson with his daddy's dark hair and his mamma's stormy blue eyes. Kid was going to be a real killer in a few years time, no doubt. He threw his arms up and Huntley managed to bend down from her position on Grayson's lap to pick Hunter up. They looked like the perfect little family, and I wanted nothing more than to experience it. I came close to it, once.

"I think it's time to feed our little man," Huntley said, kissing Hunter's forehead.

We all got up, and I was grateful to have the attention taken away from me. Huntley walked outside with Hunter, and I was about to follow when Grayson stopped me.

"Would you mind staying a little longer," he asked. "I wanted to talk to you, but after everyone else has left."

"Sure," I replied. "Is everything okay Gray?"

He gave me a small half-smile and wrapped his arm around my shoulders. "Yeah, it's fine." I didn't believe him, but decided not to press the issue. I'd wait until later.

****

I was sitting on the back steps of the porch. Grayson's parents left a little while ago, and Huntley's uncle and aunt followed shortly afterwards. We'd spent the day eating good food, chatting, and finalizing the plans for Huntley and Grayson's wedding. I laughed for the first time in months, feeling completely at ease and at home with the people around me. I was nursing a bottle of water when the deck creaked behind me, and Grayson's big body bent to take a seat on the steps next to me. He sighed and brought his all-knowing eyes to me.

"You have fun today?" he asked. I knew he was stalling but I allowed it. "I did," I replied honestly. "You don't have to worry about me anymore Gray. I'm okay. I'm getting better."

"I know, but - "

"But nothing," I interrupted. "I'm okay, Gray. This is going to be the best week of your life, and the last thing I want is for you and Huntley to spend it worrying about me."

"You're family Dem, we always worry about you. I will never understand how difficult the last few months have been for you and I'm sorry that you had to even go through it at all but Huntley was right there with you, feeling everything you felt. It killed me to see you girls hurting so bad knowing there was nothing I could do. I wanted nothing more than to kick Brody's ass for leaving but I couldn't. I didn't want him to think I was choosing sides." It was the first time Grayson was talking to me about this, and I was more than a little surprised. "I should've spoken you sooner," he continued, looking somewhat sheepish. "But I didn't want to upset you."

"Are you talking to me now because Brody is coming tomorrow?" I asked quietly.

"I need to make sure you're going to be okay seeing him this week. If not, I'll phone him right now and tell him to stay in Chicago."

My heart warmed at Grayson's thoughtfulness and I wondered what I'd done to deserve a friend like him. I was just me, an average Southern girl who had been to hell and back in the last year, and for some reason God blessed me with this amazing, loving family. It wasn't a flesh and blood family, but it was family all the same.

"You don't have to do that," I sighed. "He deserves to experience the most magical day of your life with you. We've all been friends for too long to let what happened with us come between that."

"If you don't want him here, just say the word Dem and he won't be here. I don't want you to feel uncomfortable, because then I'll get hell from Huntley and we all know how that works out for me."

I chuckled then, knowing he was right. Huntley could be a real hellcat when she was pissed, or unhappy. We'd managed to avoid Bridezilla so far, we weren't about coax it out now.

"I'm going to be just fine," I replied. I wrapped my arms around his bicep and rested my head on his arm. "He's not the only one responsible for our mess, Gray. I was also wrong."

I felt Grayson kiss the top of my head and it was comforting. I was terrified as all hell to see Brody, but I tried hiding it as best I could. This week wasn't about me. It was about two of the most amazing people I knew pledging their lives and hearts to each other forever. I wasn't about to let my problems ruin that.

"Are you going to tell him about... you know?" Grayson asked hesitantly.

Thinking about what I had to tell Brody made my chest tighten, and my throat start to burn. I tried to will the tears to stay away, but it was hard. I'd been doing so well but there were some things that would still cut me up.

"I don't know," I sniffled, trying to be quiet. I didn't want Huntley to hear me, or see me if I started crying. This felt like a set back of sorts but I knew I'd have to tell Brody *everything* at some point. Not only did he deserve to know but it was important for me to get this closure. I wasn't going to heal otherwise.

"He deserves to know," Grayson murmured, reading my mind. "It won't change what happened but it will make it a whole lot easier on you." I wasn't entirely sure that was true but he was right to some extent. Brody deserved to know what happened after he left.

"I have something else you need to know." I looked up at Grayson, and the expression on his face worried me.

"Brody might be bringing someone with him," he said. He watched me carefully, and I had no idea what he was expecting to see on my face.

"I know," I replied. Grayson looked surprised but didn't ask me how I knew. I wasn't ready to tell him anyway, even if he had asked. "Your brother will be on my arm," I said, trying to sound unfazed. "Brody can bring whoever he wants."

Grayson looked skeptical and probably thought every word coming out of my mouth was bullshit. He wasn't wrong.

"So you and my brother, huh?" he smirked. I smiled, a real genuine one at that and ducked my head a little.

"I don't have to tell you what's been going on with us," I said. "I'm sure Jeff has been keeping you up-to-date."

It was Grayson's turn to chuckle. "It's the only way I can find out how you're really doing. I know you don't always tell us everything."

"I wasn't lying when I said I was doing better, Gray. Sometimes I just need to talk to someone who won't pity me. Jeff is that person, and I really care about him."

"We don't pity you, Dem," Grayson argued. I shook my head.

"Yeah, Gray, you kinda do. You guys have looked at me like I'm broken beyond repair for too long, and I didn't want to end up resenting you for it. Besides, I had to pull myself together on my own. I may not be completely there yet, but I will be."

"You've always been strong, but it's alright to lean on someone every now and then."

"That's why I have your brother," I replied quietly, thinking about just how much Jeff had helped me.

"Okay you two, it's late and I need to put the little monster to bed." Grayson and I both looked up to find Huntley smiling at us with a sleepy Hunter in her arms. Grayson helped me up, and I walked over to Huntley. I kissed Hunter goodnight, and Huntley passed him to Grayson. I said goodnight to him too and Huntley walked me to my car.

"Are we still on for tomorrow?" Huntley asked, stifling a yawn.

"Of course," I replied. "I can't wait."

"Me neither," Huntley replied. "You drive home safe and let me know when you get home, okay?"

"It's like ten minutes."

"I don't care. I won't sleep until I get that message from you saying you're home safe." Huntley yawned again and I knew she'd fall asleep before I even pulled into my driveway. But I agreed just to appease her and hugged her goodbye before climbing into my car and driving home. After locking up and activating my alarm, I grabbed my kindle e-reader and got Coco settled on my bed. I started reading a new romance novel but it wasn't long before my eyes dropped closed and the flash of Brody's face haunted my dreams.

chapter three

8 Months Ago

DEMI

The plane touched down at O'Hare International airport in Chicago and I woke with a start. I was groggy from the flight even though it was only two hours long at the most. My mood had worsened considerably but I chalked it down to why I was here in the first place and told myself to suck it up. The sooner I saw Brody and got this out of the way, the sooner I could go home and crawl back into the darkness and despair that had been my life for the past two months. It was easier that way, for me at least. I knew everyone at home, including Huntley, had become frustrated with my behavior and my need to hide away from the world. Too bad I didn't care. They didn't understand what I had gone through and they sure as hell had no idea what it was like to live in the perpetual darkness that had consumed me. I was only a fraction of the person I once was and no one could pretend they knew what that was like.

I grabbed the small bag that I'd brought with me for my two and a half day visit from the luggage carousel and made my way out to where the cabs were parked. It was late and the sun had just started setting but it felt like I'd been awake for days on end. Everything hurt. My head, my arms, my legs, my belly. But nothing compared to the hurt I felt gnawing away at my chest. But I was here for a reason, a purpose, and I had to see that through before I allowed myself to be overcome by my grief. I hailed a cab and after sliding in, I gave Brody's address to the cab driver. As we weaved through the streets, the tall glass buildings whizzing past, it hit me that all of this was what he'd left me for. While I took full responsibility for allowing him to leave and chase his dreams, it felt like a slap in the face to know this was what he'd been chasing. My stomach twisted and I rubbed at the dull ache. I had to do this. I needed closure and Brody deserved to know the truth. Minutes later, the cab stopped outside an apartment building and I asked the driver to wait for ten minutes before he drove away. I wasn't sure how this was going to go and if necessary, I needed an escape plan. Not that Brody would hurt me. I was more worried about the pain I was about to inflict on myself. The cool evening air nipped at my skin and I hugged my sweater closer for warmth. I was always cold lately but it seemed worse with the cooler temperatures in the city. I took the crumpled up piece of paper out of my pocket that Grayson had given me and checked which apartment number belonged to Brody. If I was right, I would've been able to see which apartment was his from the street and taking a chance, I counted four floors up and six apartment windows to the right. I lost my breath when I saw him standing there, leaning against a window. Wearing nothing but what looked like his pajama bottoms, he still looked as impossibly beautiful as I'd remembered. He was the villain in my nightmares night after night and still I missed him fiercely. I stared at him for a short while, until a tall blonde came up from behind him and wrapped her arms around him. He hadn't pushed her away, but he hadn't returned her intimate embrace either. It became obvious to me then, standing outside on the sidewalk. He'd moved on. After only two months. Two months that had been nothing short of Hell on Earth for me. Just like that, life landed its' final blow, and what was left of my broken heart shattered. Tears burned my eyes and I welcomed the sting. I'd convinced myself that somewhere along the way I'd done something to deserve this, that this was the price I had to pay for how my relationship started with Brody. This was Karma's way of righting my wrongs, of restoring balance after I cheated on my ex-boyfriend, Tommy, with Brody. Clearly having Tommy beat the crap out of me when he found about me and Brody wasn't enough. Brody and the blonde disappeared from the window and I had the sudden urge to throw up. The acid in my stomach climbed up my throat and I spun around and grabbed ahold of the nearest garbage bin just in time before the fowl tasting liquid spewed from my mouth. I heaved until there was nothing left but my hollow sobs and when I had no fight left in me, I climbed back into the cab. I'd known it was a bad idea to come here. I felt it the minute I'd got on the plane back home. But against my better judgment I'd ignored the alarm bells in my head and came anyway. And I wasn't any better off for it. The cab driver looked at me as if I was mad but I ignored it. I need to get the hell out of here and fast. I only had one option. Jeff Carter.

****

"Hello?" Jeff's voice came through the phone and I'd never

been so relieved to hear it. Jeff Carter was Grayson's older brother by two years, but he was also one of my childhood friends. He'd known I was coming but a small part of me had hoped I wouldn't need to call him.

"Jeff? It's Demi." I swallowed audibly and tried to control my emotions long enough to stop the waterworks.

"Are you okay?" he asked, his tone thick with concern, "why does it sound like you're crying?"

I ignored his rapid-fire questions and skipped to why I'd called him in my time of need. "Are you at home?"

"Yes. What happened, Demi?"

I sighed, struggling to put a coherent sentence together between my hiccups and my constant blubbering. My voice was hoarse and my throat raw. "Can I come see you? P-please? I don't want to be alone right n-now." It sounded like a desperate plea and I didn't care. I needed someone. Anyone.

"Of course," he replied. "Where are you?"

"I'm leaving Brody's apartment now. What's your address?"

Jeff gave me his address and I recited it to the cab driver.

"I'll be waiting for you outside," Jeff said.

"Thank you."

It didn't take us long to stop outside Jeff's apartment building and true to his word, he was waiting for me outside. I paid the cab driver and as soon as I was free of the cab, I launched myself into Jeff's body. I cried into his chest and instead of complaining, Jeff simply rubbed up and down my back and hushed me until I was calmer. He picked my bag up from where I'd dropped it and tucked me into his side before taking me upstairs.

"I'm s-sorry," I stuttered, wiping my face. "I didn't m-mean to just s-show up like t-this."

Jeff sat me down on his sofa and looked at me with concern

in his eyes. "I knew you were in the city this weekend," he replied softly. "Grayson called. Said you'd probably call me if something went wrong with Brody."

"Oh God," I groaned between sniffles. "You must think I'm a pathetic woman. I didn't have anyone else - "

"I'm glad you came to me," Jeff said, cutting me off, "And no, I don't think you're pathetic at all. Can I get you anything before we talk about what happened at Brody's?"

"Water would be nice, thank you. And some headache pills if you have."

Jeff nodded and disappeared into his kitchen. I hardly noticed anything around me except the view he had of the city. It was dark and the city lights lit up the breathtaking horizon, showing off Lake Michigan in the distance. The sofa dipped next to me and I turned to take the glass of cold water out of Jeff's hands. I swallowed the pills he gave me and hoped that the throb in my temples would subside sooner rather than later.

"You ready to tell me what happened?"

I looked into Jeff's eyes and found what I had been sorely lacking since the day Brody left. Safety. I trusted Jeff, more than I trusted anyone at that time, and when I was sure I could handle reliving the last few weeks, I told him everything. That had been the start of something new, and something that had meant more to me than I thought possible after what I'd endured in just eight long, painful weeks.

chapter four

Present Day

BRODY

I took a seat in the crowded waiting area at O'Hare airport in Chicago and waited patiently for them to call our flight. I was heading home to Breckinridge, Alabama for my best friend Grayson's wedding. It was only a week away but they had a number of smaller events planned preceding the big day. It had been a year since I left and sometimes it was difficult to comprehend how much had happened in the short time I had been gone. Sienna took a seat next to me and handed me a cup of coffee before curling into my side. I once again acknowledged, rather bitterly, that having her next to me felt wrong but I allowed it because it filled a hole. A hole I'd been living with for the past twelve months and a hole that would become far more obvious the minute I arrived back in my hometown. I'd achieved everything I'd hoped to when I arrived in Chicago last year, and while most people would dream of my kind of success, I hated the man it made me. Sienna squeezed my hand and again it felt wrong. I looked into her brown eyes and like many times before, compared their color to the explosive green ones I'd spent my entire life in love with.

"You okay, baby?" she asked, giving me a smile. Her long blonde hair was tied up in a pony tale high on her head and I found myself wishing it would somehow magically change to the fiery red color that fueled my demons and haunted my dreams. I got myself into quite the situation as far as Sienna was concerned. She was my boss's daughter and somehow she found her way to my bed. Admittedly, it was only six months ago, and while I'd spent the majority of our semi-relationship being riddled with all-consuming guilt, she temporarily soothed the loneliness that threatened to drown me. I got hopelessly drunk one night and after she took pity on me, I spilled my guts and told her how I had lost the love of my life. It hurt to think about Demetria and how broken we'd left things, which is why having someone like Sienna was so…*convenient.*

"Yeah," I replied. "Just anxious to get home and see everyone." And Demi. Part of me wondered if bringing Sienna with me was a good idea but at the same time I didn't want to attend Grayson and Huntley's wedding alone. Jeff would be Demi's date but I was still worried that she'd moved on and if I had to be subjected to seeing her with someone else then I at least I wouldn't have to be alone. Sienna curled deeper into my side but it felt wrong to wrap my arms around her so I didn't. Instead, I pulled my phone from my pocket and dialed Grayson's number. He answered on the second ring.

"Hey bro," he greeted happily. "What's up?"

"Nothin' much, just waiting to board the plane and get my ass home," I replied.

"Yeah man, we're looking forward to seeing you. Hunter keeps asking when his uncle Brody is going to be here, it's driving me crazy."

I chuckled, smiling at the thought of my Godson.

"I can't wait to see the Lil' man either."

Grayson clears his throat and the other end of the line filled up with a somewhat awkward silence before he spoke again. "Is Sienna with you?" he asked hesitantly. The tone of his voice did little to cover his concern.

"Yeah, why?"

"Listen man," he began. "I've booked you into a hotel for the week. You know we're doing renovations to the ranch, so you can't stay there. I made reservations under your name until you leave on Sunday."

"I thought we were staying with you and Huntley?"

He sighed heavily. "That was the plan, but Huntley…" he hesitated.

"Huntley what?"

Grayson muttered 'shit' on the other end and I was pretty sure he was brushing his hands through his hair. I'd seen him do it a thousand times. "Huntley doesn't want you staying here with another woman," he said. "I guess she's still pissed about everything and she doesn't want any drama before the wedding."

I responded with a sigh of my own and had difficulty suppressing my anger. Huntley was fiercely protective of Demetria and I granted her that but I was tired of being made to feel like the villain. I was also hurt. Hell, I was still hurting. I'd just learned to live with it.

"Alright Gray," I said, giving in. "Send me the check-in info and I'll stop by at your place once we've arrived."

"I'm sorry," he replied. "I tried reasoning with her but fuck, she's stubborn and I didn't want to fight with her over this shit so close to the wedding. She's been stressed enough as it is."

"Don't worry about it. I understand. I know you guys were caught between a rock and a hard place when all that shit went down with Demi and me. I get it."

Sienna looked up at me, a frown between her eyes. She watched me carefully while I spoke to Grayson. "Thanks for being cool about it and again, I'm sorry you have to crash in a hotel. You can stop by for a drink once you're settled, I'll be waiting." The fact that he didn't invite Sienna to their house didn't go unnoticed but I understood and chose not to make an issue of it.

"Yeah bro, I'll see you later."

Grayson said his goodbye and I ended the call before slipping my phone back into my pocket.

"What was that about?" Sienna asked, staring at me.

"Nothing," I lied easily, avoiding her gaze. "We're staying at a hotel. Grayson will send me the check-in info when we land and then I'll go and say hi, maybe have a drink with him." I didn't bother asking Sienna if she was okay with this plan because I didn't care. As far as I was concerned, having her here was a means to an end, a place-filler. Nothing more. She stayed quiet and went back to reading her magazine while I tried my hardest not to think about how hard the week ahead was going to be.

****

After arguing with Sienna, I left her at the hotel and took a cab to Grayson and Huntley's house. My truck was parked in their garage so I'd just use it to get around this week. The cab came to a stop and I paid the driver quickly before making my way to the front door. Before I could knock, the door flung open and Hunter launched himself into my legs. Grayson stood there smiling.

"Bwody!" Hunter squealed, squeezing my legs.

"Hey Lil' man," I replied, picking him up. He'd grown so much since I last saw him and it was hard to believe he was already two years old.

"Hey man." I greeted Grayson with a fist bump and walked through the house. Grayson followed me out onto their outside deck and grabbed us each a beer. I took a seat with Hunter in my lap and Grayson followed suit on the opposite side of the table.

"It's good to see you man," Grayson said. He took a pull of his beer but kept his eyes trained on me. I knew that look. He was trying to read me, see how I was doing since the last time he saw me. He had nothing to worry about but I didn't say it.

"Yeah, you too. You ready to be a married man?"

He chuckled and grinned widely. "I was ready the day Hunter was born, but Huntley wanted to wait until she graduated, so I told her we'd do it soon after."

"Speaking of Huntley," I said, taking a pull of my beer. "Where is the bride-to-be? I was hoping to see her."

Grayson looked down and shifted uncomfortably. That only meant one thing. I wasn't going to like his answer.

"She's with - "

"Demi," I said, finishing his sentence.

"Yeah," he replied. "Something about a girls night."

"Or she's avoiding me," I said.

Grayson sighed and pulled his hands through his hair, a clear sign of both frustration and resignation. I felt bad for the guy. He was caught between his fiancé and his best friend, albeit unintentionally.

"Huntley cares about you," he began. He finished off his beer and put the bottle down before sitting back into the chair. "And I don't think you should take her behavior personally.

She's just trying to make sure Demi is going to be okay being around you again after everything that happened."

"Like you're doing with me," I stated.

His smile was crooked when he replied, "Exactly."

My chest tightened thinking about Demetria, and how much she must've been hurting for Huntley to feel the need to side with her. A mixture of guilt, anger and self-justification swirled in my chest. Next to my grandparents, Demetria was also my only family and I was never able to imagine a life without her. But then I made a choice and ended up leaving her behind. I destroyed her, and in the process tainted everything that we had. It was something I regretted every day and being back home with the possibility of seeing her made me nervous. I'd been thinking about it for days and I couldn't decide if she'd be willing to let me fight for her.

"The ranch is looking good," Grayson remarked, breaking into my thoughts.

"I'm anxious to see how much progress they've made with the building," I replied. Grayson and his brother, Jeff, each bought a third of the ranch I inherited after my twenty-second birthday, and they'd agreed to help me fix it up. My grandparents still lived in the old farmhouse I'd grown up in and as soon as the new house was done, they would move in. I hadn't decided what I wanted to do with it yet, but we'd agreed it would always stay in the family. Hunter dropped off my lap and ran around to where Grayson was sitting. Grayson picked him up and he settled against his chest. Seeing Grayson with his son made the ache in my chest a little more real. I wasn't jealous of Grayson, but I wanted what he had - an amazing woman to come home to every night and children who made up the most perfect parts of us. I wanted that with Demetria, I always had. I always would. But in the same breath, I worried that it would never happen for us and I blamed myself. I'd walked away.

"I'd better get going," I said. "Looks like you need to put the little monster to bed."

Grayson smiled and looked down at Hunter. He'd dozed off at some point.

"I'll wait for Huntley to get home," he replied. "She should be back any minute."

Just then the sound of a lock echoed and boots clicked on the hardwood floors. I looked up just as Huntley appeared at the door, and stood to greet her. Her smile was warm as she approached me, but I could see indecision swirling in her eyes. Could I blame her for being cautious with me? I'd broken her best friends' heart and I probably would've felt the same if I were in her shoes.

"Hey Brody." She hugged me and I was once again reminded of her grace. I wasn't her favorite person, I hadn't been for a while now, but she still treated me as if I were a friend. I returned her hug, replying, "It's good to see you again."

When she pulled away, Grayson appeared at her side and bent his head to kiss her. I looked away, feeling somewhat uncomfortable with their display of affection. It was a painful reminder of what I'd had and recklessly thrown away for something that no longer meant anything to me. I cleared my throat, and their heads whipped up as if remembering that they weren't actually alone.

"I'm going to take off," I said. "But I'll see you again tomorrow."

"I'll walk you out," Huntley said. I nodded, bumped fists with Grayson while he cradled a sleeping Hunter, and made my way out their home. I was dying to know how Demi was doing but I was almost sure I'd forfeited that right. In the end, my need to know outweighed everything else. I turned to face Huntley, and found her regarding me. It was both a knowing and probing gaze.

"How is she?" I asked, letting it slip out before I lost my nerve. Huntley's eyes pinned me and her lips thinned into a straight line. She was wondering whether or not to tell me and I hoped to God she took enough pity on me to tell me what I wanted to know.

"I honestly don't know," she replied quietly, taking two steps closer to me. Her eyes lowered for a minute, and when she brought them back to me I could tell she wasn't lying. "Some days it's hard to tell, really. She does a pretty good job of hidin' things. Too bad I know her better than that."

I brushed my hands through my hair, and my chest deflated with a heavy sigh. I could read between the lines.

"That bad, huh?"

"Why do you suddenly care?" Huntley asked, anger lacing her usually sweet voice. I was caught a little off-guard by the strength of her tone.

"I've always cared," I replied quietly, silently pleading that Huntley will believe me.

"You have a really funny way of showing it, Brody. You left without a word, and she had to deal with…" Huntley clamped a hand over her mouth quickly before finishing her sentence. Something in the way she said that didn't sit well with me. Not at all.

"Deal with what?"

Huntley remained quiet, and I watched her eyes glimmer with unshed tears. "Deal with what?" I asked again, my tone harder and more persistent than before. I stepped closer and Huntley's hand shot up to stop me.

"I can't," she whispered. "I've already said too much."

"Huntley, please - "

"It's not my story to tell," she said quickly, interrupting me.

"Then why bring it up?"

"Because I want to be pissed at you, Brody," she huffed.

"It's been a year and you're only *now* asking how Demi is doing. To top it off, you decided to bring your fuck buddy with you to our wedding. What is the matter with you? Don't you care about Demi at all anymore? It's bad enough she has to see you this week and now she'll have to deal with seeing you *with someone else.*"

I wanted to tell her she was wrong, that I'd called Grayson every day for three months after I'd left to find out if Demetria was okay. What she didn't know is that Grayson stopped telling me. He'd even started ignoring my calls until I'd stopped asking altogether. It killed me. Huntley's words only ripped open the old wound all over again. Leaving me with nothing but the guilt I'd carried in my heart all this time.

"I'm sorry Brody." Huntley shifted from one foot to another, and looked away as if she could no longer stomach the sight of me. For the second time, I couldn't blame her. "But you really fucked up. My only hope is that you and Demi will somehow find your back to each other and have what Grayson and I have. I want that for you two more than anything." Huntley's eyes conveyed everything I had feared and the realization that I had truly fucked up hit me square in the gut. With those parting words, Huntley stretched on her toes and placed a kiss on my cheek. At least she didn't hate me, that much I was sure of, and as I watched her walk back on their house, I had the nagging feeling deep down in my bones that the damage I'd left behind a year ago was far greater than what I'd previously thought. It only left me with more questions, the most obvious being *Can I make it right*?

chapter five

Huntley

I closed the door behind me and let out a breath. The week leading up to mine and Grayson's wedding had barely started and I already felt like I was dodging bullets. I hated being nasty to Brody but I was still angry with him. I didn't care if I had no right to be after a year had passed. He destroyed my best friend and left us to put her back together. I shook my head, laughing at my own ridiculousness. I didn't need to get involved with Demi and Brody's drama a week before I married the love of my life. It was bad juju.

I walked upstairs and stopped to check on Hunter. My little man was sprawled across his bed, hair in every direction. He'd kicked the blankets off the same way Grayson did when he got hot. He was so much like his daddy it was scary. My life hadn't turned out as I expected and even though we had Hunter really young, he was the best thing to ever happen to us. I couldn't regret him, not even for a second.

I was leaning against the door when two strong arms slid around my waist. Grayson's scent engulfed me, and I relaxed into his hard chest. "You ready for bed?" he asked quietly. I yawned, causing him to chuckle. "I'll take that as a yes."

"Sorry." I yawned again. "I'm wiped."

"I'll run you a bath." Grayson kissed my head, and I watched him walk down the hallway to our bedroom. He looked over his shoulder, a smirk on his face. He knew I was watching him. When he disappeared I quietly snuck into Hunter's room and switched off his Scooby-Doo nightlight. I kissed his forehead and inhaled his sweet scent. I loved him so much my heart burst. When I walked into our bedroom, Grayson was standing at the basin in his cotton drawstring pajama bottoms with no shirt. I don't know why he bothered though. He preferred sleeping naked. I padded over, slipping my boots off along the way and hugged him from behind. I kissed him between his shoulder blades and pressed our bodies together, loving the feel of his warm skin against my cheek. After spending the day with Demi, I was tired. Grayson twisted to face me and I held on tighter.

"Everything okay?" he asked. He tilted my chin up with his forefinger, and looked at me thoughtfully.

"I think so," I replied. "It was a long day."

He nodded thoughtfully and pushed away from the counter. He rubbed our noses together, giving me an Eskimo kiss. "Lift."

I lifted my arms, smiling. He loved undressing me this way, and it always made me feel cherished. When my shirt was gone, my jeans followed, as did my bra and panties. Grayson's eyes darkened, turning luminous Jade in color. I wanted him and he knew it because he wanted me too, but he could see I was tired and being the considerate man that he was, he scooped me up in his arms and lowered me into the hot, steamy water.

"Oh God that's good," I moaned, feeling the tension in my muscles disperse amongst the vanilla and honey bubbles around me.

Grayson cleared his throat and I looked up. "What?"

He shook his head, amused. "You know better than to make those noises, baby. They drive me crazy."

"Sorry," I replied, blushing. "It does feel really good."

Grayson straightened and I unabashedly stared at his perfection. He'd become a little bigger since graduation, his muscles more defined. His work at the Sports Rehabilitation Centre at Whitley University kept him fit and I liked it. I liked it a lot.

"You can't look at me like that." Grayson's voice was rough with a husky undertone that only appeared when he was aroused.

"Like what?" I asked innocently, knowing very well the kind of look I was giving him.

"Like you want me."

My mouth tipped up as I continued to look at Grayson from beneath my lashes. "I always want you, Gray." It was true. My physical need for him was never satisfied, no matter how many times or how many ways he took me.

He bent down again, making us eye level. He touched my face, and despite the hot water, I shivered. "You're tired," he said quietly, rubbing the circles under my eyes that were no longer hidden by make-up. "But I'm always up for a late night cuddle."

I laughed lightly, falling in love with him all over again.

"Sounds perfect," I sighed. As much as I wanted to get sweaty with my soon-to-be husband, I was tired. I'd been napping a lot lately.

Grayson kissed me and stood. "Enjoy your bath, baby. I'll see you in bed."

I nodded and watched him walk out before sinking into the hot water. The feeling blooming in my chest, in every molecule of my body, was one I'd become accustomed to and yet I still reveled in it every time it washed over me like it was the first time I was feeling it. Contentment. True untainted contentment.

GRAYSON

Huntley sighed and curled deeper into my side. Her head was on my chest and my arm was wrapped around her waist. We were only a few days away from our wedding and it often felt like it had taken us forever to get here. After Hunter was born, Huntley took some time off school while I started working on getting the Sports Rehabilitation Center at Whitley. When the time was right, Huntley finished her degree and started counseling at the elementary school here in Breckinridge a few days a week. I was so proud of her. She was determined to achieve her goals and still be the best mother to our son. I smiled then, thinking about our two year old just down the hall. I couldn't wait to fill this house with more kids. Little girls who looked just like Huntley.

"What's got you smilin' like that?"

I looked down and found Huntley's green eyes peering up at me. My heart skipped a beat, the same way it always did when I looked at her.

"I'm happy," I replied. "And I can't wait to make you my wife."

Huntley's eyes glistened and in them I saw the world. She was my world. Our family was my world.

"Don't cry," I murmured, wiping her cheeks.

"Don't mind me," she whispered. "It's been happening a lot. I seem to leak when I'm happy these days."

I chuckled. "You're happy?"

"Deliriously."

"Well I must be doing something right then."

Huntley smiled and I kissed her lips. "I wanted to ask you something," I said. I'd been thinking about this for a while, but the timing just hadn't felt right with all the wedding planning and such.

"Of course, baby. Anything."

I swallowed, feeling nervous. God, this woman tied me in knots. "I think we should try for another baby."

I held my breath and watched as Huntley's eyes widened. "I mean if you're ready," I added quickly. I didn't want her to feel pressurized if having another baby wasn't something she wanted just yet. I could understand if she wasn't ready but I was praying to God that she was. There was no better time in my life than when Huntley was pregnant with Hunter. Seeing her belly grow with my baby was something I desperately wanted to experience again. The room filled with silence, and then it was broken by nothing but a whisper.

"Okay."

My heart leapt from my chest and I slid down next Huntley so that our faces were only inches apart.

"Okay?" I asked, wanting to hear it again.

Huntley gave a small nod and I captured her mouth in a long, deep kiss.

"Say it," I murmured against her lips, "tell me we're having another baby."

I felt her lips tip up and then she said it. "We're having another baby."

Those were the sweetest words ever spoken. And then we were done talking.

chapter six

DEMI

We sat in the small yet opulent bridal boutique situated two hours outside of Breckinridge. The wedding was only three days away and it was the final dress fitting for all of us. Grayson's mother, May, sat to my left and she was deep in conversation with Huntley's aunt Emma as we waited patiently for Huntley to come out. Until now, the only person who had seen Huntley's dress was her aunt and I was anxious to see how she looked. I envisioned her in something form-fitting with a slight flare at the knees and a chapel length train. Not that it really mattered what she wore. She'd make a black garbage bag look fantastic.

The shop assistant brought us some more champagne and I took the flute from her hand gratefully. I had an uneasy feeling in the pit of my belly and I was determined to squash it with more bubbly goodness. The last thing I wanted was to ruin this day for Huntley with my less than exuberant mood. It's not that I wasn't excited but my mind was preoccupied with other things. Huntley had texted me last night and told me that Brody was in town and knowing that he was here stirred so much inside me that I found myself thinking about our past, about things I'd rather forget but never will. I could lie and say I didn't want to see Brody but I'd only be fooling myself. I wanted to cast my eyes on his beautiful face and look into the depths of his deep chocolate brown eyes. I wanted to know what the past year had been like for him and if he had hurt as much as I had. I wanted to know if he thought about me, about us, every day the way I did, if he had trouble sleeping because it was my face that kept him awake. I wanted to see if he had changed at all, or if he was the same man I gave my heart to when I had little understanding of just how much he'd come to mean to me. I wanted to know if he'd see that I had changed, that he had changed me and that despite all that we had put each other through, he was the still the keeper of my broken, yet still beating heart.

A gasp brought me back to the present moment and all thoughts of Brody vanished when I turned to see Huntley walk out of the dressing room and onto the raised platform in front of us. It was impossible to describe how beautiful she looked without comparing her classic looks to that of a Greek goddess. Her tulle and satin gown, with its romantic silhouette, was white with ivory all-over lace and lace applique. It had capped sleeves that accentuated her toned arms, and a deep v-shaped neckline that complimented her curves. It was nothing short of exquisite.

"Well?" Huntley's voice broke the silence and I heard the slight tremor.

"You look…" May started but couldn't get the rest of her

sentence out and I understood why. Huntley looked … *breath-taking.*

I stood up and walked over to where Huntley stood, waiting.

"It's perfect," I whispered, feeling my eyes well up with tears. "You look like a princess and I can't think of anyone more deserving."

Huntley swiped away a few tears and stepped down from the raised platform. "Thank you," she whispered. I smiled and hugged my best friend, feeling my heart swell. I was so happy for her but a small part of me wondered if it would ever be me in a beautiful gown of my own. Emma and May came up to Huntley and we all shared a few more tears.

"Grayson is going to fall over when he see's you, sweet-heart," Emma said, grinning wildly like a proud mother. "Your mamma would've been proud and I wish they were here to share this magical time of your life, but they're in your heart and taking it all in with you."

I felt a pang of sadness and couldn't even begin to understand how not having her parents here must've affected Huntley.

"Thank you Aunt Em," Huntley replied quietly. "I'm so happy and I know they can feel it from wherever they are."

"We're all taking it in with you, baby girl," May added while holding Huntley's hand. I'm sure anyone walking past the boutique window would've thought we were crazy but we were simply sharing a moment that would only happen once. Huntley and Grayson had the kind of love everyone hopes to find but rarely do. I still held out hope that some day it would be me.

Huntley turned to look at me and smiled. "I have a surprise for you."

I frowned, wondering what she could be talking about. She

nodded at the shop assistant who disappeared for a short while before returning with another garment bag. Both Emma and May shared knowing glances and I knew they must've already known about this.

"What's going on?" I asked. The assistant unzipped the garment bag, and pulled out another beautiful gown. I stared in confusion.

"I had this made for you," Huntley said, taking the ornate dress from the assistant's hands. It was far more beautiful than the dress we had originally chosen and I was almost drooling at the sight of it.

"But we had a dress picked out?"

Huntley's mouth tipped up. "I know but you're my Maid of Honor and you needed something more appropriate. So what do you think?"

"I love it," I replied, holding the dress.

"Well don't just stand there," Emma laughed. "Go try it on!"

I squealed on my way to the dressing room and slipped the dress over my head after taking off my clothes. I didn't bother looking at myself in the mirror before stepping out. I smiled widely when I saw Huntley's reaction and giggled when Emma and May started fawning over me. I stepped in front of the raised mirror and looked at the girl staring back. Although I knew she was no longer a girl. Life had taken that away and had left behind a fraction of the person I used to be.

"It's stunning," I said quietly, admiring myself. It was a one shoulder, full-length gown, Champaign in color. It was ruched across the breasts and accented by a black band around the waist with a diamante flower detail on the side. Huntley came to stand next to me, and put her arm around my shoulders. "Now you look like my M.O.H."

****

Huntley and I were in the car on our way home after having lunch with her aunt and Grayson's mother. We'd been singing along to Taylor Swift's 'Red' album for over an hour and spent a great deal of that time laughing at how terrible a singer I was. Huntley turned the music down and I found her regarding me carefully.

"You'd tell me if you weren't okay, right?"

I shifted in my seat and faced her. "Of course I would, but why do you ask?"

She sighed and looked at me quickly before returning her gaze to the road ahead of us. "I'm... I just..." she stuttered.

"C'mon, spit it out, we don't have all day."

"I'm worried about you, that's all. Brody's back in town, which you know and Grayson and I already had a fight about him--"

"Why would you be fighting about Brody?" I asked, interrupting her.

"Well," she hesitated briefly, but I wasn't sure why, "for some stupid reason Grayson decided to tell Brody and his...his... bed buddy that they could stay with us this week. When I found out, I lost my shit and threatened to withhold my goodies from Grayson unless he fixed it."

I stared at Huntley, my mouth open. "Your goodies?"

"Yeah," Huntley replied, blushing. "No sex."

An unladylike giggle burst free from my mouth and I laughed. "You threatened to take away sex all because Brody was going to stay with you?"

"Not just Brody," Huntley defended. "He brought his sex toy with..." her words trailed off as realization flashed in my eyes. My brief laughter died and I felt my heart sink. Brody had really moved on. Deep down I knew it, I saw it with my own eyes once but I never thought I'd have to face it again. "Shit," Huntley muttered. "I'm sorry Demi."

I shook my head, struggling with the sick feeling in the pit of my stomach that had been hovering over me all day. "You didn't have to do that," I said quietly. "You should've let them stay with you."

Huntley's eyes looked as if they were about to pop out of their sockets. "Have you completely lost your mind?"

"No, but it would've been the right thing to do considering he's Grayson's best friend."

"Well that's too bad because you're *my* best friend and after what he did to you he can go sleep in a lice infested bush."

I chuckled but it was an empty sound. "You'll have to let go some time," I said. "He wasn't the only one at fault." I stopped myself before I brought up the fact that I was hiding something from Brody, something that would undoubtedly change *everything*.

"I don't care," Huntley retorted. "I don't want a stranger around my son and I sure as hell don't want that woman near us, or you. It's a good thing Grayson knows what's good for him, because I hear Brody and his attachment are now staying at the hotel in town."

I went quiet. I had no idea what to say because thinking about Brody with someone else was hard enough. I didn't need to talk about it too.

"I should've kept quite," Huntley sighed. "I'm sorry. I know you'll tell me if something's wrong and you know I'll be there the whole time if you need me."

"I know. Can we maybe talk about something else though? Like where you think Grayson is taking you for your honeymoon."

Huntley's face lit up and our previous conversation evaporated as she got talking about their honeymoon.

"I think we might be going somewhere exotic," she said. "Grayson says I must pack as little clothes as possible."

"That has nothing to with an exotic location and everything to do with spending your entire honeymoon in a bed."

A blush crept up Huntley's neck and settled in the apples of her cheeks, causing me to laugh. "Don't be modest now," I said, smiling. "I lived with you remember?"

"How could I forget," Huntley giggled. "You reminded me on several occasions how loud I am."

"You know I believe he's doing something wrong if you're not screaming."

Huntley squirmed and I stifled a laugh. "Oh my God, you're totally thinking about having sex with Grayson right now aren't you?"

Huntley ducked her head but not before I saw her cheeks redden further. I muttered "lucky bitch" under my breath. Unfortunately Huntley heard.

"Maybe Jeff can help you out with that," she teased. I felt my face warm and tried to act nonchalant. But the truth was, when it came to Jeff Carter, I was anything but nonchalant.

"Not this again," I whined, pretending to be annoyed. I was happy to talk about Jeff. He'd become the perfect distraction and kept my dark, unhappy memories at bay.

"Just admit that you like him and we won't talk about him anymore."

"I'm not admitting to anything," I replied, crossing my arms across my chest. "Besides, I don't think Jeff see's me that way. We're just good -"

"Friends," Huntley parroted, finishing my sentence for me.

"We've had this discussion before," I said, feeling slightly exasperated.

"I know, I know, but I think there's more to it than you've told me and I'm just trying to figure the two of you out."

Of course she was right and I felt guilty that there were some things she didn't know about my relationship with Jeff. Or more importantly how it all started.

Huntley spoke before I could think about it too hard. I looked up in time to see that we had arrived back in Breckinridge, and had already stopped outside my house.

"When I've figured it out I'll let you know," I commented.

"Thanks for today," Huntley said after a few minutes of silence. "I had fun."

"Me too and thank you for my gorgeous dress."

"I'm happy to do it for you, Dem. I love you like a sister and I'm really glad that you're going to be the one up there with me."

She sniffled and I handed her a tissue. "Sorry," she said, wiping her nose. "I've been feeling emotional lately."

"It's fine, no one would blame you. You're allowed to be a total mess this close the wedding. It's practically a requirement."

Huntley laughed lightly and bent over the middle console of her Jeep to give me a hug. I squeezed her tight. "I have a favor to ask," Huntley said as she pulled away. "I was hoping you'd be able to look after Hunter one night this week before the wedding. I have something special planned for Grayson."

"Of course, I'd love to keep him for the night. You don't even have to ask. Just show up."

"You're the best," Huntley sniffled again and I couldn't help but wonder what the hell was wrong with her. It was more than just pre-wedding emotions but I couldn't put my finger on it. I said goodbye and made my way inside. When I opened the door Coco started yapping and jumped up against my legs. "Poor baby," I cooed. "I'm sorry I left you alone today. I missed you." I bent down and picked the chocolate bundle up, laughing when she licked my face. I kicked off my shoes and walked into the kitchen where I fed Coco and poured myself a glass of Chardonnay. It was perfect for the summer heat. I plugged my phone into my docking station and listened as the sweet sound of my favorite female country singers filled the room. Jana Kramer sang about calling the love of her life 'Whiskey' and the Dixie Chicks crooned about cowboys. I was so absorbed in the music that I didn't even hear my doorbell ring, or the door open. I turned around to refill my glass and found Jeff watching me, his mouth tipped up into that half grin.

"Jeff!" My glass barely made it onto the coffee table next to the sofa before I threw myself into his arms. He caught my body and I felt his broad, muscular chest rumble beneath me. I inhaled his cologne and savored the scent that had come to represent safety and comfort.

"Hey Red." The deep, rich timbre of his voice met my ears and I hugged him tighter. I smiled at the mention of his term of endearment attributed to my long fiery red hair. He'd been calling me 'Red' for a while and I'd be lying if I said I didn't like it.

"I've missed you," I whispered against his neck.

"I've missed you too."

chapter seven

Demi

I slid out of Jeff's arms and looked up into his green eyes. They were warm and welcoming and familiar. His dark brown hair was shorter than the last time I'd seen him but it still hung in his eyes. His features reminded me of Grayson, except they were sharper and more defined. He smiled, making his eyes crinkle at the sides, and all my troubled thoughts and feelings vanished.

"When did you get here?" I asked, unable to fight the grin on my face.

"About twenty minutes ago," he replied. "I wanted to come see you first."

"I'm glad you did." I hugged him again, and felt my heart jump into my throat. Something was different about this. The butterflies taking flight in my belly were a testament to that.

Pushing those thoughts aside, I pulled Jeff further into my living room. "Can I get you a beer?" I offered, knowing he'd probably need a cold one after his flight.

"That sounds great," he replied, following me into the kitchen. I grabbed a beer and turned around just in time to see Coco fall at Jeff's feet and roll on to her back.

"When did you get the pup?" Jeff asked, amused. He bent down and started scratching her fuzzy belly and let out a laugh when her leg started twitching.

"Two months ago," I replied. "She keeps me company."

Jeff stood and Coco waddled over to her dog bed in the living room. When I passed Jeff his beer, his eyes were watching me carefully. He took my hand and led me outside onto the deck. He knew my house like the back of his hand and he was one of two people who had a spare key. I trusted him that much. He sat down on one of the loungers and pulled me between his legs, settling my back to his front. The position was very intimate but I found myself relaxing into Jeff's body like I belonged there. It was a gorgeous summer night and the stars above us created a very romantic backdrop. It wasn't the first time I wondered what it would be like to be more than just friends with Jeff but I knew it would still be a while before I even considered it. I just wasn't ready.

"I can hear you thinking from here, Red," Jeff murmured in my ear. "You want to fill me in on everything I've missed since I last saw you?"

"You know everything already," I replied, smiling. "We talk on the phone all the time."

Jeff took a sip of his beer, and I turned my head to look up at him. His throat worked as he swallowed and I had a difficult time not biting my lip. "Our last call was three days ago," he said. "What's happened since then?"

I laughed and turned my head, resting it on his chest.

"Really?"

"Yeah, really. Tell me *everything*."

I shook my head with a laugh, incredulous. "We had Huntley's final dress fitting today, and she had a new dress made for me."

"Remind me to thank her," he said around the rim of his beer. "Apart from the bride, I'm going to have the most beautiful girl on my arm for sure."

I swallowed hard and my face warmed from his compliment. It wasn't the first time he'd said I'm beautiful but like the atmosphere between us, something about it felt different. The butterflies in my belly flapped gently and excitement settled in my bones. I realized that what I was feeling for the first time in months was *alive*.

I shifted and turned my body to face Jeff. His eyes met mine and the silence stretched out between us. We weren't talking but our eyes communicated everything we were too afraid to say.

"I'm really glad I'm going to have you there with me," I said quietly, looking down at my lap. My admission came without thought and it made me more vulnerable in front of Jeff than I had ever been. But I wasn't scared. I wanted him to know that he meant something to me, even if I wasn't entirely sure about what that was exactly. He tipped my face up with his index finger and gave me the trademark Carter lopsided grin.

"Me too." His voice was deceptively soft and I fought the urge to shiver. "I'm not going anywhere."

"That's not true. You'll be back in Chicago soon."

Was I disappointed that he'd be leaving in a few days? Did I want him to stay? Or did I want him to stay with *me*?

Jeff cleared his throat. "Actually..." he paused, "I was thinking of moving back home in a few months."

"What? Why? You love your job and you love Chicago!

Why would you come back?" As much as I wanted him to say I was his reason for coming home, because I was that selfish, it scared me. I took a deep breath and quieted the voices screaming in my head while Jeff struggled with the ones screaming in his.

"I loved it," he said. "But something's missing and I think it's time to come home."

I heard the loneliness in every word that left his mouth and more importantly, I understood it. I felt it too, lived with it every day. I'd even learned to accept it because really, what other option did I have?

"I know what you mean." I looked down, unable to keep looking into Jeff's green eyes. There was a long pause

"Have you seen him yet?"

Jeff's question caught me off guard and I frowned, not liking the way I knew this conversation was headed. "No but I have a feeling it won't be much longer. I know he's here."

"When was the last time you saw him?"

I bristled. This conversation was getting really old and I was getting tired of trying to convince everyone that I was going to be just fine. The problem was I couldn't tell if I was trying to convince them or myself. "The last time was when I flew to Chicago to tell him about…" I trailed off, unable to get the words out of my clogged throat. Jeff cupped my cheek and like so many other times before, his touch comforted me, brought my troubled heart some form of peace and assurance that everything would be okay.

"You're the strongest person I know," he murmured. "Brody has no idea what he lost when he left you here."

"You think too much of me, Jeff." I was unworthy of this man and he didn't even know it. His body moved closer and when I looked up, our faces were merely inches apart. I waited for my heart to race and thump wildly in my chest. It never happened and I tried to reason that it didn't matter. But I was lying. I wanted someone who could get my pulse running wild like…

"I think you're beautiful and kind, and stronger than you give yourself credit for," he inched closer and my breath hitched, "and I think I want to kiss you."

My heart stopped and my brain switched off. It had been so long since I experienced the feel of a mans lips on mine.

"Okay," I breathed. I closed my eyes and held my breath, waiting to feel Jeff's lips against my own.

Just then, the shrill sound of Jeff's phone ringing pierced the air and we froze. I opened my eyes.

"Dammit," Jeff muttered, making me smile.

"You'd better get that," I replied quietly. "Your brother probably thinks I kidnapped you."

"I'd be a willing captive, Red."

My heart stuttered back into a steady rhythm and Jeff kissed my forehead before pulling out his phone to answer it. I hopped off the lounger and took the empty wine glass and beer bottle inside. I stood at the basin, rinsing my wine glass when I saw a shadow standing on the sidewalk. I squinted into the darkness, feeling a familiar chill settle over my skin. A car drove past, illuminating the lone figure. Brody. I stilled, locking eyes with the man who put my life back together only to rip it all up. My heart raced, making my body thrum. I hadn't felt that when Jeff touched me, or even when he kissed me. No. This feeling my body reserved for only one person. I dropped the wine glass, shattering it as I walked to the front door. I ran down the steps, but when I searched for Brody he was gone. Had he been watching me all this time? Did he see Jeff here? I rubbed my arms even though it was hot and walked back inside.

"Everything okay?"

I jumped and turned to find Jeff standing behind me.

"Yeah," I replied. "Thought I saw something outside. You take care of your phone call?"

"It was Grayson. He wanted to know when I was going to arrive. Sounded a little pissed when I told him I came here first but he wasn't surprised. I think I'd better go before he comes here to get me himself. My taxi will be here soon."

"That sounds like Grayson," I giggled.

The sound of Jeff's shoes echoed on the floors as he stepped closer.

"There's one last thing I have to do before I go," he murmured.

"What's that?" I asked, my voice equally soft.

"This." Jeff's hand came around my neck and he brushed his lips across mine before capturing my mouth. He traced my bottom lip with his tongue and before I could worry about the consequences of this moment I allowed him in. My body relaxed into his embrace and savored the feel of his hands on my body, the way he caressed me gently and coaxed my mouth into following the slow pace he set. Our tongues danced and he licked every part of my mouth, learning it, enjoying it. He pulled away before I was ready and I whimpered at the loss of heat. His forehead came to rest on mine and when my eyes opened again I found him looking at me.

"Hmmm," he sighed, "that was good as I'd imagined it."

"You've imagined kissing me?" I squeaked.

"I sure have."

I stretched onto the balls of my feet and placed a sweet kiss on Jeff's cheek. He was an amazing guy, but now that he'd kissed me I recognized the absence of...*fire*. He didn't make me feel like I was ready to explode from a kiss alone. He didn't make my nipples bead beneath my bra or heat pool between my legs. I didn't feel the need to rip his clothes off and touch every inch of flesh that covered what I knew to be an amazing body.

The excitement I'd felt earlier was misplaced, probably mistaken for the longing to feel a man's touch. It was my heart that dropped, leaving me wondering if I would ever have that again or if I was meant to live without it.

"Goodnight, Jeff."

Jeff brushed my cheek and gave me a peck on the mouth. "Night, Red."

The door clicked behind him and as always, I was left alone with nothing but my own guilt for company.

****

Sleep didn't come easy that night. I tossed and turned, fighting with the villains in my head. It wasn't kissing Jeff that had kept me awake though. It was the guilt that I'd felt as soon as he'd left, the feeling that I'd betrayed Brody in some way. It was idiotic. Brody had moved on so why couldn't I?

You know why, the voice in my head said, reminding me that I knew exactly why moving on, even a year later, had been almost impossible. Sure, I liked how Jeff made me feel, but it just wasn't the same. I'd only compare him to Brody. In fact, I'd compare *every* man to Brody and then be disappointed when they come up short. I sighed. I was exhausted and my mind had been running a mile a minute all night. Having had enough, I threw my comforter off my body and climbed out of bed. It was already eight in the morning so I decided to throw on my running gear and hit the road. Coco wasn't too pleased, but I gave her a treat and snuck out the front door. I needed something to get my feet moving and when Miley Cyrus' 'Wrecking Ball' started playing, I almost tripped over my feet. *How appropriate,* I thought. I turned up the volume and picked up my pace, hitting the back roads that wound around town. It was hot and I was sweating like a hooker in Church but it felt *so good*. The burn in my muscles surged me forward until I thought my lungs were going explode and by the time I made it into town I was ready to collapse. I walked past the stores, greeting the townies as I passed, and stepped into Emma Morgan's bakery. The cool air blasted my skin and I sighed in relief and appreciation for the reprieve. I'd only been out for an hour but it was long enough. Huntley's aunt saw me and smiled while motioning me over to the counter.

"Morning, sweetheart. What can I get you?"

"Hi Mrs. Coach. Coffee and a water please."

She started getting my coffee ready and I watched the other patrons come and go in a steady stream of bodies. The bell chimed above the door, only this time it made me freeze. I had my back to the door but I didn't need to look to know who had just walked in. The air became thinner and I found it difficult to breathe. The hairs on the nape of my neck were standing at attention and I had to force my body not to run into those familiar arms. Emma looked at me with sympathy in her eyes and that was all it took to confirm that I was right. I turned around slowly and even then, there was no way to prepare myself for what was in front of me. Brody was smiling down at a gorgeous blonde woman, giving her his rapt attention. Hell, *I* couldn't even help staring at her. She had a red dress on, synched at the waist, which showed off her long, bottle-tanned legs and delicate waist. Her platinum blonde hair was tied up in a high ponytail on top of her head, showing off her high cheekbones, pouty pink lips and perfect nose. She was gazing at Brody with bright eyes the same way I had done before. With love and adoration. It wasn't her expression that caught me though. It was his. His smile, the way he looked at her, seemed real, like he meant it. *Oh God, this can't be happening.* I took a moment to take him in before this all went to hell. His hair was a little shorter and he still wore it in that *just fucked* way. I swallowed, wondering if it looked that way because of *her,* because she'd run her slender fingers through it while he made her scream out in pleasure. The voice in my head shouted *'GET OUT!"* and at that moment Brody decided to look up. Our eyes locked and small amount of air I'd managed to get into my tired lungs was knocked out.

"Demetria."

Brody said my name like it was a treasure, like he needed to protect it. He was the only person who ever used my full name, even when we'd made love he'd called it out. It unraveled me. I stood frozen for a brief moment until my brain started shouting commands and my legs moved. In my hurry to get away, I smacked into the waitress walking past me and we ended up in a heap on the floor. Brody's *girlfriend* snickered behind her perfectly manicured fingers, while I prayed for a hole to appear in the floor that would swallow me. The front of my tank top was covered in cold coffee and under normal circumstances I would have gagged but my need to flea overpowered every other useless thought bouncing around in my head. I muttered "sorry" to the waitress, ignoring her scowl, and scrambled my way out of the bakery. I walked as quickly as I could and yet fate felt the need to prolong my torture just a little bit longer.

"Demetria, wait!"

Really? He couldn't just let me get away? I huffed and spun on the heel of my running shoe, missing his chest by millimeters. I could smell his cologne and recognized the scent easily. It was a bottle of Ralph Lauren 'Polo Blue' and it smelled like clean, fresh water mixed with Brody. It was my favorite on him.

"What?" I snapped. I didn't care if I should've been more polite because I sure as hell didn't feel like being *nice*. It had everything to do with seeing Brody again after all this time and making a complete ass of myself, but it also had to do with how easily he got me riled up.

"Weren't you going to say hi?" he asked, a hurt look on his face. What? *He's* hurt?

"No, I wasn't. You looked a little preoccupied and I was hoping you wouldn't see me."

Brody sighed and pulled his fingers through his hair. Part of me was relieved because that small action meant he was the one who mussed up his own hair, not that stupid blonde bimbo.

"I knew you were there before we walked in and what you saw with Sienna wasn't at all what you think it was."

I crossed my arms over my chest and stuck my chin out defiantly. "It doesn't matter what I thought, Brody. I know you're with someone else. I was just hoping - " I stopped myself before I said something I would regret. Seeing him with someone else was killing me inside, so much so that I had no idea how I was still keeping it together with him standing so damn close. But I didn't want him to know that I was hurting, I was too proud to let him see that. So I put on a front and pretended that I didn't care at all. The only problem with that was I didn't know what hurt more - seeing him with someone else or pretending that I didn't care.

"Are you with Jeff?" he snapped, trampling all over my thoughts.

I gasped, remembering that it was Brody who I saw standing outside my house last night.

"It was you," I said quietly. "Why were you there?"

"I wanted to see you, so that we could avoid something like this, but when I got there I saw you inside with Jeff and - "

"He's a friend and if he were any more than that it would have nothing to do with you. You have no right to anything in my life anymore." My throat thickened at the last part and I knew it was a partial lie. There was still too much he had a right to know but I just wasn't ready to tell him. I wasn't sure if I would ever be ready. Brody stared at me and I saw the hurt and anger swirling in his brown eyes.

"You know what, I can't do this right now," I said, breaking eye contact. "I apologize if you were offended, but you knew it would be like this when we saw each other. I don't know what more you want from me."

Brody snorted and I looked up to see him glaring. He was about to speak but I stopped him. "You'd better get going," I said, peering around his body. It was a little bigger than I remembered, his arms and chest a little more defined. Malibu Barbie was spiting daggers in my direction with her eyes. "Your girlfriend clearly knows who I am, and doesn't like that you're talking to me."

I turned to leave but Brody's hand wrapped around my upper arm and he pulled me into his chest. My body's reaction was immediate, like it was natural instinct to be that close to him. "I don't give a fuck about her, Demetria. This conversation is far from over."

With that, he turned and left, stalking down the sidewalk. I sucked in a lung full of air as if I'd been deprived of it and walked away on shaky legs. That didn't go nearly as bad as I had expected but it had shaken me enough to wonder if I could handle being around Brody at all.

chapter eight

BRODY

"Did you have to do that?"

I turned to look at Sienna. Her arms were crossed over her chest and she was scowling. I was still reeling from seeing Demetria again and almost forgot that Sienna was there.

"Do what?" I asked, confused.

"Run after your ex like a dog in heat," she snapped. Irritation swirled in my chest and collided head first with the part of me trying not to put Sienna back on a plane back to Chicago. Having her here would only complicate things.

"I didn't run after her," I replied harshly. "I had to speak to her."

Sienna huffed and for the first time she looked more like a petulant child, rather than the sophisticated businesswoman I had come to know. I asked myself what I ever saw in her to begin with and the answer was the same as it always was: she filled a space and soothed the constant ache, even if it was temporarily.

"I don't like that."

I resisted the urge to throw my head back and laugh. "I don't care. I told you I'd have to talk to her at some point while I was in town. Now stop pouting like a baby and get over it, Sienna. You have no say in whether or not I speak to her. It would be best if you remember that."

I walked past her, ignoring the glare she threw my way, and walked into the coffee shop. Huntley's aunt, Emma, was standing behind the counter and I knew she'd been watching the encounter. The look in her eyes told me she wasn't at all pleased with me. Little did she know that no one could be more displeased with me than I was with myself. I should have stayed in Chicago, even if it meant missing Grayson's wedding, but the chance to see Demetria after so long was too alluring to pass up.

****

I stopped my truck outside the old farmhouse that was my home growing up and climbed out. Sienna had been giving me the silent treatment all day and for once the silence didn't bother me. She could stay in my truck for the rest of the afternoon for all I cared. I wasn't exactly looking forward to introducing her to my grandmother anyway. I knew they wouldn't get along. That might've had more to do with the fact that my grandmother adored Demetria and thought no other women would ever be better for me. I didn't disagree, but I couldn't exactly tell Sienna that. I took a walk around the front of the house to the porch and that's when I noticed Demetrias' red Lexus.

"Ah hell," I muttered. "This isn't going to end well." I heard the sound of footsteps behind me and the uneven click of heals on the dirt told me I didn't need to look back to know it was Sienna. She followed me up the porch steps without saying a word and came to stand at my side while I knocked on the door.

"It's open." My grandmothers' voice still sounded the same and hearing it brought a smile to my face. I opened the screen door and walked in, not bothering to make sure that Sienna was following me. When I walked into the living room I found my grandparents in a heated discussion. They both stopped talking as soon as they saw me.

"Brody!" my grandmother, Luanne, gasped and rushed towards me. She wrapped her thin arms around my waist and hugged me. I relaxed and felt the familiar sense of safety the comfort of her arms had always given me as a child. I kissed her grey hair that was tied up in a neat bun and returned her embrace.

"I'm so happy to see you," she whispered. The hitch in her voice made my chest ache. I'd missed her so much and carried so much guilt for leaving them. Luanne Scott was an incredible woman and I could not have asked for a better mother figure.

"I've missed you, Gama," I replied. My grandfather, Clay, cleared his throat and I looked up to find him watching us. His eyes were glossed and he looked thinner and more tired than I'd remembered. My grandmother let me go and wiped her tears. "I'm a silly woman," she sniffled. "I shouldn't be getting all emotional like that." I rubbed her back as my grandfather stepped closer. He pulled me into a strong hug and it took me a moment to return it. I was a little shocked. Clay Scott wasn't an affectionate man, unless it came to my grandmother. But something about the way his big arms engulfed me made me feel like the six year old boy again, the one who had to accept that his parents didn't want him. "Good to have you have you home, son."

I pulled away and held him at arms length. "You too, Gramps. You look good for an old man," I joked.

He laughed and my smile only broadened. "Who have you got here?" he asked, looking past me. I turned to see Sienna watching us rather awkwardly. She was a duck out of water here and it only made me question my decision to get involved with her. Her eyes told me she was pissed, but she plastered on a fake ass smile and stuck out her hand. "I'm Sienna," she said, shaking my grandmothers hand. My grandmother's expression was laughable and I could tell she wasn't impressed by Sienna. Unlike most people, my grandparents weren't as easily charmed and the only person who had managed to win them over was Demetria. "I'm Brody's girlfriend."

I froze, my thoughts of Demi halting at the term Sienna used to describe herself.

"It's nice to meet you dear," my grandmother said politely. I knew better. As soon as she had the chance she was going to lay into me.

"I've heard so much about you," Sienna said, reaching to shake my grandfathers' hand. Her tone was clinical and detached, like this was a business transaction rather than a sincere introduction to two of the most important people in my life.

"That's funny," my grandfather replied, looking Sienna in the eye. "Because we've heard nothing about you."

She gasped, and I sucked in a laugh. My grandmother slapped my grandfather's chest, but the need to laugh was etched in the wrinkles around her mouth. Sienna politely excused herself, spun on her heal and stormed out of the house, muttering curse words under her breath.

"Thanks Gramps," I groaned. He shrugged and replied,

"Not my fault the stick up her butt leaves no room for a sense of humor." I chuckled because well, it *was* funny, and walked outside to find Sienna. My foot hit the second step of the porch when a scream pierced my ears. I knew that voice anywhere. I ran around the side of the house where the barn was situated, and increased my pace when I saw Demi rolling on the ground with Jeff on top of her.

"NO!" she screamed. "Please, Jeff! NO! STOP!"

I couldn't see her face but seeing her with him made my blood boil in the worst way. I didn't want another man touching her, whether I had a right to feel that way or not. I grabbed Jeff's shoulder and hauled him up to his feet.

"Brody, what the - " Jeff's words were cut off by the sound of my fist making contact with his jaw and his body hitting the ground. He jumped up quickly and tackled me to the ground. The wind was knocked out of my lungs and I barely had enough time before Jeff's knuckles hit the side of my face. Demi and Sienna started shouting at us but we didn't stop. I rolled us over, straddling Jeff's waist, and hit him again. The faint crack of his nose should've stopped me, but all I could think about was his hands on Demi and my rage bubbled over. Two strong arms wrapped around my chest and pulled hard enough to get me away from Jeff. I looked over my shoulder and saw Grayson holding me back. I was so focused on smashing Jeff's face that I didn't notice Huntley and Grayson had pulled up to the farmhouse.

"Oh my god!" Demi yelled, scrambling to where Jeff was lying on his back. He had blood running down his nose and over his mouth. If Grayson didn't look so pissed I would've been happy that I'd just broken his brother's nose for no reason. "Are you okay?" she asked him. The way she looked at him with concern made my anger rise and I had the urge to punch him again.

"Yeah," Jeff replied, wiping his nose with the back of his hand. "I'm fine." Demi helped him up and I hated it.

"What the hell is wrong with you?" Demi asked me. "What did you do that for?"

"What the hell is going on here?" my grandfathers voice boomed and we all turned to see him approaching us.

"Let me go," I growled at Grayson.

"Not if you're planning on hitting my brother again," he replied angrily.

I shook my head. "I won't."

Grayson let go of me and took a step towards Jeff. "Let's get you cleaned up," he said. He gave me a look of disapproval. "We'll talk about this later, Brody."

I watched them walk to the house and disappear inside. I was left alone with my grandfather and Sienna.

"You want to tell what that was about?" he asked. The disappointment in his voice hung heavily in the air. I couldn't explain my way out of this one. While I knew I'd fucked up, I couldn't regret it.

"No, sir," I replied.

He snorted and shook his head. "I'm no fool, son. A man could be blind and still see what made you fly off the bandwagon for no rhyme or reason. I suggest you and your *friend* get going," his disliking of Sienna didn't go unnoticed but I'd expected it. He disliked anyone who wasn't…

"You've worn out your welcome for today." Just like that my grandfather had dismissed me and I knew I deserved it. He'd always taught me that a man who used his fists to solve his problems was not a man. Sienna stalked towards the car and slammed the door as soon as she climbed in. Great. Now I had to deal with her bullshit too. I was about to make my way towards the car when I saw Demi storming down the porch steps and headed straight towards me. Her red hair flew in all directions and her face was screwed into a scowl, but all I could think was that I'd never seen a sexier woman in my life. I should've felt guilt, having Sienna waiting for me in the car, but she was the last person I truly cared about.

"You have some serious balls," Demi said, hitting my chest with her forefinger. I watched in amazement as she went off on a tirade.

"What the hell is your problem? You broke Jeff's nose!"

I grabbed her arm and dragged her around the other side of the house until we were both out of sight. She glared up at me and my eyes dropped to her mouth and then her heaving chest. I stepped forward and before I could second guess myself, I did the one thing I knew I couldn't resist. I kissed her.

chapter nine

DEMI

Brody's mouth crushed mine and while my brain shouted at me to stop, my body responded the only way it ever would when it came to Brody. His tongue traced the seam of my lips and I opened up for him, allowing him to explore the contours of my mouth. His hand came to rest at my nape, while the other cupped my hip and pulled me closer to him. What we were doing was wrong, but I couldn't rationalize it that way when my heart believed it was right.

Everything else around me disappeared as my blood started humming in my veins, making me feel feverish. Brody moaned into my mouth and in that moment it felt as if he was breathing life into me. I inhaled, swallowing his scent greedily, silently begging for more. But I knew *more* with Brody would never be enough. I'd learned that very early on. I had no doubt that his kiss alone made my panties wet and slick with desire. My breasts grew heavy and tender, aching for his touch. It had been so long and my body knew it. I experienced a total loss of control around Brody, which only made stopping that much harder. It was when his lips left a hot, moist trail down my neck that reality came crashing down. What was I doing? I pulled away, breathless with swollen lips.

"You shouldn't have done that," I said, my voice shaky and quiet.

"I wasn't the only one enjoying it," he retorted with a smirk. My hand came up, poised to slap him, but he grabbed my wrist before I could. "Now now, there's no need for violence."

"That's rich," I bit out, suddenly angry. "It's okay for you to punch whoever you want for no Goddamn reason, but when I want to then I'm being violent."

Brody leaned in close, our noses touching. "He had it coming."

"So did you! What possessed you act like such an asshole, Brody?"

"Like you'd believe me." His voice softened, as did his eyes.

"Try me," I replied, "because from what I saw, you hit him because you felt like it!"

He had the decency to look sheepish when he replied, "I thought he was…hurting you."

I snatched my hand out of his grasp and took a much-needed step back. My head was swimming from our heated kiss and the anger I started to feel bubbling its way to the surface.

"Hurting me? Are you fucking kidding me right now? He was *tickling* me!"

Something on Brody's face changed and his expression became unreadable. It was unnerving. I'd always been able to read him, no matter what expression was on his face. The face looking back at me was blank, and I hated it. More than I'd ever admit, even to myself.

"Forgive me for wanting to *protect* you," Brody sneered. My kiss-induced haze had completely evaporated and only white-hot fury remained. Who the hell did he think he was?

"You lost your right to protect me," I said harshly, glaring at him. "You walked away and it was Jeff who was there when you weren't!"

Brody's face fell and for a brief moment I felt the need to take the words back. If only taking words back was enough to erase our past. Nothing with Brody and I had ever been that easy.

"I will *never* stop protecting you," Brody ground out. "God Himself couldn't stop me."

"God might not, but I sure as hell will!"

With that, I brushed past Brody and walked back into the house without a backwards glance. I was upset, and I squeezed my eyes shut to stop the sudden onslaught of tears threatening to spill. I found everyone in the kitchen and when I walked in their gazes landed on me. It made me uncomfortable, like I was under a microscope, and I immediately worried that they knew what Brody and I had been doing outside.

Grayson had cleaned Jeff's face, but he was still holding a dishcloth under his nose.

"Are you okay?" I asked Jeff, feeling both concerned and embarrassed.

"Yeah," he replied. "Did he leave?"

I looked down, and nodded, unable to look him in the eye. I was afraid that my kiss with Brody was written all over my face.

"Did he say anything to you?" Huntley asked. She was leaning against the kitchen counter, arms crossed over her chest.

Brody's grandparents stood to the side, but they were also watching me with a keen interest. If anyone in the room knew if something happened with Brody it was them. Apart from Grayson and Huntley, Luanne and Clay Scott had also become family, and even after Brody left I remained close with them. Close enough to have them know what happened when Brody left. Close enough to trust them to keep it from him. Jeff and I stopped by the ranch so that he could show me what plans they had for the land, since Grayson and Jeff had each bought a third of the property. Brody's grandparents would live on the property for the rest of their lives, and the ranch would then stay between Brody, Grayson, and Jeff's families. They were family anyway, so it made perfect sense. Of course, we hadn't been expecting Brody and his new girlfriend to show up.

"He…" I hesitated, squirming uncomfortably where I stood, "he said he thought Jeff was hurting me. That's why he punched him."

"What did you tell him?" Jeff asked. His voice carried a hint of agitation and I couldn't tell if it was with me or Brody he was agitated with.

"What do you think?" I asked, not doing anything to hide my own sudden irritation. "I told him the truth."

"Is he still here?" Grayson asked. He stood up and looked ready to throw his own punches if Brody was still on the ranch. It was a rare occurrence, if not non-existent, to see him want to punch his best friend.

"No," I replied, completely exasperated. "And what's with the inquisition? It's not my fault he hit Jeff!" I turned around and walked back outside onto the porch. I needed some fresh air and there was nothing better than inhaling country air. The land in front of me went on for what looked like miles and the setting sun provided an exquisite landscape. It really was beautiful. I'd always imagined living here with Brody, surrounded by our children and horses and blue skies. It had always been my dream, my fairytale. But like most little girls who dream of such things, I'd learned the hard way that fairytales are nothing more than child-like ideologies.

The screen door closed behind me and I looked over my shoulder to find Brody's grandmother, Luanne, watching me. She came to stand beside me and started out at the open space in front of us. I had a tremendous amount of respect for this woman. She was short, with a slender build, but like most women from her generation, she was a force to be reckoned with. When Brody's parents abandoned him, his grandparents were tasked with raising a very angry six-year-old boy who had a jaded perception of what life was like. He'd been damaged and yet somehow, amongst all the rubble left behind by his parents, Luanne and Clay had managed to give him a stable, loving home. It was because of them that he'd been the man I fell in love with during college.

"You want to talk about it, sweetheart?" she asked me quietly. Something in her voice was knowing.

"I just..." I stopped. I didn't know how to tell her how I was feeling when I didn't know myself. When I continued, my voice sounded small and again I hated that it was because of Brody and how he made me feel. "I didn't mean for any of that to happen," I gestured to the door, "I didn't know Brody was going to be here."

"No one blames you, sweetheart, but that's not what I was referring to."

I frowned. "Then what did you mean?"

"I meant the reason you looked so flustered back there." Her mouth tipped into a small smile and I knew I'd been caught. She saw me kissing Brody.

"I..." I snapped my mouth shut. I couldn't explain my way out of this one and there was no way I would ever lie to

Luanne. She laughed briefly before turning her worldly eyes to me.

"It's alright, sweetheart, I won't rat you out. I just want you to be smart, and think about the other people you could hurt while you're trying to make sense of things between you and my grandson."

"There's nothing between me and Brody," I replied quietly.

Luanne touched my hand in a reassuring gesture and I had the feeling I wasn't going to like what she was going to say. But I listened anyway because I trusted her.

"I'm old, but I'm not blind," she chuckled. "You and Brody will find your way to each other again. You might be a little lost right now, but in the end, he's your destiny, as you are his."

"What makes you so sure?" I asked curiously.

She looked away momentarily, lost in thought. "Almost forty years ago, I was you and Clay was Brody. We lost our way but I knew in my heart of hearts that he was my past, present and future."

"What happened?"

"We weren't ready," she replied thoughtfully. "We still had to become the people we needed to be to make each other truly happy. We met other people and after three years of messing around with those relationships, we realized that it all began and ended with us, me and Clay. There was no one else in the world for me."

"And you think it will work out that way for me and Brody even after everything that's happened?"

"Sweetheart, nothing will keep you apart if it's meant to be. Clay drives me crazy and we fight like hell on wheels, but I refuse to live without him. You can live without Brody, but when you decide don't *want* to live without him, then it will all fall into place. In the mean time, be careful you don't hurt Jeff in the process."

I shook my head and replied, "I would never hurt him. We're just friends."

"Does *he* know that?"

"I'm not sure what you mean."

"Sweet girl, that man in there," she pointed in the direction of the kitchen, "is so in love with you and he has no idea that your heart is still unavailable."

I was about to disagree when the screen door opened. Huntley stepped out.

"I'm sorry, did I interrupt?"

Luanne smiled. "Not at all, Huntley dear. We were just talking." She winked at me and squeezed my hand. "Give it time sweetheart, Rome wasn't built in a day."

She disappeared inside and left me alone with Huntley.

"Everything okay?" she asked. I was getting tired of hearing that from everyone but I knew it came from a good place.

"No," I replied honestly, "but it will be."

She nodded and I was grateful when she didn't press the issue. She knew I'd talk to her when I was ready. I just needed some time to sort out everything in my head, especially Luanne's last observation about Jeff being in love with me. I still hadn't decided how I felt about it.

"Are you still okay with looking after Hunter tonight?" Huntley asked.

I smiled. "Of course. I can't wait."

"Great," Huntley replied. "We're getting ready to go."

"Alright. I'll be right behind you."

Jeff decided to get a ride with Grayson and Huntley and while it stung that he was angry with me, I used the drive home to think. It was time I started sorting out the mess in my head.

chapter ten

HUNTLEY

Grayson had been broody for the rest of the afternoon and I could tell he was still brewing over everything that had happened at the ranch. We'd dropped Hunter off at Demi's house for the night, and Jeff had taken off to visit his parents. It was supposed to be our last romantic night alone before the wedding and Grayson was sulking.

Our house was quiet for the first time in months and while the sound of Hunter's laughter filling every room brought me so much joy, I was looking forward to spending some much-needed alone time with Grayson. I walked into the living room and found Grayson watching some sports reruns. I sat down beside him on the sofa and curled into him.

"Can I make you something to eat?" I asked.

"Whatever you feel like is fine with me, babe."

I rolled my eyes and stood up. "You know, Gray, sulking isn't a good look on you."

I walked to the kitchen and started pulling out some ground beef and pasta to make lasagna. After a few minutes of silence, I felt Grayson standing behind me and he wrapped his arms around my waist. He kissed my neck and murmured, "I'm sorry."

I turned around and faced him, our bodies pressed together. "It's okay to be mad," I replied, "but I'd rather you talk to me than stay quiet."

He sighed. "It's just frustrating to be stuck in the middle all the time."

"I understand," I replied. "I just think that Demi and Brody are dealing with a lot and as their best friends we have to help them any way we can. After everything Demi went through this past year I can't imagine how difficult it is to see Brody again, especially knowing she's keeping so much from him. Your brother is unfortunately caught in the crossfire."

"What if Demi hurts Jeff? Then what?" I understood Grayson's concern for his brother, and I couldn't say that I wasn't worried either. The entire situation was far more than complicated and someone was bound to get hurt.

"Your brother is a big boy," I replied with a small smile. "No matter what happens, he'll be okay. This is between him and Demi."

"And Brody."

"They'll work it out," I said. "Now can we please enjoy our night alone?"

Grayson's eyes flashed and he grinned. "You'd better get dinner started then. You'll need your energy because I have no intention of sleeping tonight."

A shiver of anticipation moved through my blood and coiled in my belly. I stretched onto my toes and brought our mouths closer until they were only inches apart. "Me neither."

****

We ate dinner and while Grayson cleaned up downstairs, I decided to take a shower. I was expecting to feel anxiety or even cold feet now that our wedding was days away, but all I felt was peace. I had no idea my life would end up at this point the day I met Grayson but I had no regrets and the thought of spending the rest of my life with him, watching our children grow, thrilled me to no end.

I settled under the hot water and as I started washing my body I heard the shower door open. I turn my head and smiled when I saw a very naked Grayson step in. "Can I help you?" I asked, my tone light and teasing.

He smirked and my knees almost buckled at the sight. God he was sexier now than the day I met him, which I didn't think was possible.

"I don't know," he replied, feigning incredulity. "I was looking for my hotter-than-hell fiancé. Maybe you've seen her? Blonde hair, stormy blue eyes, body that can bring an entire army to its knees?"

I shrugged. "No, I don't think so, but I'd be more than happy to help you with whatever it is you need."

I turned my body towards him as he stepped closer and let out a gasp when he picked me up. "I'm not sure," he nipped at my lips, "she can never know."

I smiled, squirming when the tip of his rigid cock pressed at my entrance. "I won't tell her if you won't."

"It'll be our little secret." He groaned and pushed into me. I sucked in a harsh breath at his welcomed invasion and felt my body adjust to accommodate his generous size. We'd done this countless times, in every position and on every surface of our house, but every time I had him inside me felt like the first time and it only made my crazier. Hungry for more.

"You always feel so good," he murmured. He pressed me against the wall and as his hips started thrusting faster and faster, I dug my nails into his back and hung on like my life depended on it. I knew it was going to be an intense ride. It was never anything less with Grayson.

"Harder," I whispered harshly, relishing in the way our bodies slid up against each other. Without hesitation, Grayson surrendered to the wild, inhibited craving we have for each other and started pumping his hips fast and hard. My orgasm hit and left me breathless as I bucked wildly against his hips. My toes curled and I tightened around his hot length, squeezing until I knew he was close.

"Fuck," he bit out, chasing his own orgasm.

"That's the point," I laughed, still catching my breath.

His brows furrowed and his hands gripped my hips to the point I was sure it would bruise. The way he held me so tightly, yet so reverently did crazy things to me. His orgasm ripped through him and the potency was enough to trigger a second orgasm for me. This time we screamed together and found ourselves floating into oblivion.

Grayson's eyes found mine, despite the spraying water, and in them I saw my present and my future. He gave me his lazy post-orgasm smile and said, "I can't wait to call you my wife." If I could, I would've pulled him closer to me, but we were already as close as we could possibly be. There was no more space between us.

"And I can't wait to marry you," I replied.

He kissed me then, like it was my breath alone that gave him life, and for the second time in my life, my heart left my body and jumped right into Grayson's.

chapter eleven

BRODY

I knocked on Demi's front door and tucked my hands in the front of my jeans while I waited for her to answer. I'd seen her a few hours ago at the ranch and yet I was nervous. My body was still thrumming after our kiss and the prospect of seeing her again negated all my feelings of guilt over hitting Jeff.

The door opened and Demi's face was a mixture of surprise and annoyance. "Brody? What are you doing here?"

I frowned. "I'm here to fetch Hunter."

"Uh, there must be a mistake. He's with me tonight."

"Grayson asked me to take him tonight," I replied.

"Well Huntley asked me." Demi crossed her arms and quirked her eyebrow. It was her *challenge me* stance, one I had seen many, many times before.

When it started to sink in, I couldn't help but smile. A

laugh burst from my mouth and Demi stared at me as if I'd gone mad.

"I can't believe he did it," I murmured. I looked down and rubbed my neck. Grayson had orchestrated this.

"Did what?" Demi asked, confused.

"Grayson… he uh… he planned this."

"That makes no sense."

"Yeah," I sighed. It made perfect sense, but only to me. Grayson knew how badly I wanted to talk to Demi and it's just like him to come up with a way to get us together.

"I've actually just put Hunter to bed," Demi said, "I think it will be silly to wake him up now." I couldn't argue with that. It was already late.

"Right. I'm sorry to have disturbed you." I turned around and prepared to walk away when Demi's delicate hand stopped me.

"Have you had dinner yet?" she asked quietly. Now that she'd mentioned it, I was starving. Sienna decided to have dinner without me and I'd been so eager to get away that I'd forgotten about dinner.

"No. I'll get something on my way home."

"I've just made some pizza and it's too much for me to eat alone. Do you want…to join me?"

"Sure," my voice wavered, "I'd like that."

I followed Demi inside and closed the door while she headed into the kitchen. Everything about this house was so distinctly 'Demi' that I couldn't help but smile a little. It was warm, and welcoming. It was a home. Part of me ached because creating a home was something I had been desperate to do with her. When I walked into the kitchen, seeing Demi doing something as simple as placing food on our plates brought an onslaught of memories that I'd spent months suppressing. We'd spent many nights in the kitchen making food together, eating in nothing but our underwear and cleaning up the mess we made after I'd made love to her on the kitchen counter. It was impossible not to get lost in the memories that had held me prisoner in my own mind…

I lifted Demi up onto the counter and stood between her bare legs. She was wearing one of my shirts and nothing else. Her hair was a wild, red mess of waves and her eyes were bright. With swollen lips, she kissed my neck and slid her hands down my back. My sweats hung low on my hips and Demi started pushing them down with her feet. I started unbuttoning the shirt she was wearing and stopped when her pink nipples were exposed. She moaned when I sucked one into my mouth and locked her ankles behind my back, pulling me closer to her. I felt the heat between her legs and my cock started hardening immediately. Demi grinned and it was wicked. She was a naughty little minx and as insatiable when it came to sex with me as I was with her.

"You're going to kill me," I murmured. I kissed a trail from the valley between her perfect tits and stopped over her heart, smiling when I felt her pulse jump.

"There are worse ways to go," she replied, her voice rough and breathy. "I can't think of a better way to die than with you deep inside me."

My smile faltered and our eyes locked in a heated stare. Her dirty talk drove to the brink of insanity and I'd be a fool to deny how much I loved it.

"Baby, having your hot, tight little pussy wrapped around me is only one of two ways I'd want to die."

Her brows creased and I smoothed it with my thumb. "What's the first?" she asked. I held her nape and pulled her face closer to mine until we were sharing our breaths. "When we're ninety," I replied, "and old and grey and surrounded by all our grandchildren. I want to look back and see you in every memory, every moment and know that we've lived this life side-by-side, just you and me. Always."

I watched Demi's eyes glisten and kissed away the single tear that spilled over her rosy cheek.

"I didn't think I could love you more," she whispered. "You are my heart, my soul, my present and my future. Everything I have ever done, every decision I have ever made has led me here, to you. I love you, Brody, so much."

I kissed her gently and murmured, "I love you too, Demetria Rosemead, more than anything."

"Show me," she said.

And I did…

"Brody?"

I shook the memory and looked up. Demi was standing next to me, holding both our plates. "Are you okay?" she asked. I was surprised to see the genuine concern on her face.

"Yes, sorry," I cleared my throat, "I just have a lot on my mind."

Demi nodded and handed me my food. I took a sniff and hummed. "You were always good at making pizza's."

"It's your lucky night," she laughed lightly, "it's your favorite. Ground beef and green peppers with steak sauce and Mozzarella cheese."

We exchanged a look, words escaping me, and took a walk outside onto the deck. Demi sat down on one of the lounge chairs, on the left like she used to, and I sat on the right.

"It's a nice night," Demi said before taking a bite of a pizza slice. I looked up and the sight was exquisite. Thousands and thousand of stars littered the sky and it was the second most beautiful sight I'd ever seen. The first was the day I met Demi. She was wearing a pink and blue polka dot dress and I remember thinking she was the prettiest girl on the playground. The moment she threw that mud pie in my face was the moment I knew she was the one I'd be spending the rest of my life with. How had we lost that? How had I drifted so far away from that that the woman sitting next to me felt like a stranger? I'd made so many mistakes in my life, but Demetria was the one thing I got right and I fucked it up royally. All for a job I now hated and I life I *thought* I wanted.

"Are you happy?" I blurted out. When Demi's head whipped around I knew I shouldn't have said anything.

"Why would you ask me that?"

I put my plate down and turned in my seat to face her. "Because I want to know. I still care about you, Demetria." My voice came out harder than I intended.

"Why, Brody? So you can gloat about how amazing your life is without me? So you can remind me one more time that you're happy with *Sienna*? Because if you're trying to hurt me it won't work." She stood up and stormed inside. I rubbed my face and shook my head. "What the fuck am I trying to do?" I asked no one. The quiet of the night greeted me and I decided it was probably better for me to leave. I picked up our plates and made my way back inside. I found Demi in the kitchen, leaning against the counter with her back to me.

"I didn't mean to upset you," I said. I placed our dishes in the sink and turned to face her.

She snorted, spinning around. "I guess you never meant to leave either."

"Demetria, I – "

"No," she cut me off, "I don't want to hear your excuse."

"Then let me apologize." It was a plea, a desperate one. I needed her to hear me out and let me try and fix what I'd broken.

"You're a year too late." Her voice cracked and in her eyes I got a small glimpse of what I had done to her. It was enough to make me want to take it all back. But I couldn't, and now I had to consider the possibility that the little girl I'd fallen in love with all those years ago no longer loved me. It was a possibility I wasn't prepared for and never would be.

"We have to talk about this," I said, trying one last time.

Demi shook her head, her eyes red and puffy. "You've had countless chances to talk to me and I grew tired of waiting."

"What does that mean?"

She walked closer and I took a moment to really look at her. She was thinner and she had bags under her eyes. She looked tired. She looked *broken.* "It means I picked up the pieces you left behind and moved on with my life. I stopped waiting for you, Brody."

My breath faltered as if someone had knocked the wind out of my lungs.

"You're with Jeff, aren't you?"

"You lost the right to ask me that."

"Answer the question, Demetria."

"No, okay? I'm not with Jeff, but I wish I was because he's an amazing man." She sniffed and I clenched my fists to stop myself from grabbing her and comforting her.

"So what's the problem? If he's so perfect then why aren't you with him?" I half-yelled.

"Oh my God," Demi cried. She wiped her face and took a breath. "I'm not with him because my heart is taken! How can I love him when my heart will always be yours?"

We stood there staring at each other, and I tried speaking but Demi beat me to it. "There, you got what you came for right? Now I think you should leave. Please."

I swallowed hard. I had to respect her wishes. I wasn't prepared to do any more damage than I already had and judging by the look on Demi's face, it was too late. I'd fucked up again.

"Okay," I whispered. I took a risk and leaned in to kiss Demi's forehead. She didn't move or push me away. I murmured, "I'm sorry," against her forehead and saw myself out. When I climbed into my truck and hit the steering wheel until my hands hurt like hell, I realized that Demi thought I loved Sienna. She was very, very wrong.

chapter twelve

DEMI

"Can I get you a drink?" Jeff asked, yelling above the loud music. We were at Nicky's Bar for a combined bachelor and bachelorette party for Huntley and Grayson. We'd spent countless nights partying it up here during college and it reminded me of a simpler time. The interior décor and the long bar that lined two of the walls hadn't changed at all. It still smelled like beer and stale peanuts and I found I didn't mind it so much. It was proof that not everything had to change.

I wasn't really in the mood to be out but what kind of Maid of Honor bails on her best friends bachelorette party? She could tell something was wrong but I'd been dodging her questions since we arrived and at some point decided to suck it up. I'd had a sleepless night the night before and I'd replayed my conversation with Brody in my head all night, which was the reason for my less than enthusiastic mood.

"Can I have a Southern Comfort and lime, please?"

Jeff's eyebrows shot up and he looked surprised. "You sure?"

Irritation flared and I bit back the compulsion to ask him if he was my mother. "I'm sure," I replied, trying not to sound like a brat. He turned around and I watched him disappear into the thick crowd as he headed towards the bar. It wasn't his fault I wasn't good company. I looked around at all the college kids drinking and having fun like they had no cares in the world and when my gaze fell on the doors, the reason for my crap-tastic disposition walked in. Brody's sandy blonde hair looked stylishly tousled and his dark jeans clutched every part of his upper thighs, showing off the impressive package between his legs. He wore a navy blue button down shirt that he'd rolled up to expose his chorded forearms. If it weren't for the blonde woman next to him that had just about surgically attached herself to his side, I would've salivated at the sight of him.

My traitorous heart skipped a beat, despite our heated conversation last night. My eyes fell to the blonde next to him and in the dim lighting of the bar, I was sure I saw her smirk at me. She was very much a cliché with her salon dyed hair, obvious fake tits and bottle-tanned legs that went on for miles. The thought of Brody being with her baffled me, but then again, I was starting to understand that he was no longer the man I knew him to be.

He headed towards our table just as Jeff got back with our drinks and I wasted no time in grabbing the whiskey tumbler from his hands and downing my drink. The mixture of the lime and bourbon flowed down my throat and warmed my body, making the tension in my muscles ease.

"Whoa," Jeff admonished, "easy there tiger."

I smiled. "I was thirsty."

Huntley and Grayson rejoined our table and an awkward silence descended on the table. I could feel the tension between Brody and Jeff but for once in my life I didn't want to worry about it. I wanted to let go of it all. I wanted to *dance.* I ignored Brody and Sienna and looked at Huntley. "Wanna dance?"

She looked between Brody and I and then nodded, following behind me. We made our way into the middle of the dance floor and Florida Georgia Line's song 'Cruise' started playing through the speakers. The crowd shouted in excitement and soon everyone started singing along. I forgot about everything on my mind and focused on how good the beat of the music made me feel.

"I'm going to find Grayson," Huntley said into my ear. The song changed to something more upbeat and I decided it was time to hit the bar. I followed Huntley back to our table and flagged down a waitress. She brought me another Southern Comfort and lime, only this time I sipped it like a normal human being. Sienna whispered something Brody's ear, and he frowned before following her to the dance floor. She turned her head and looked at me over her shoulder, an obscene sneer on her face. Bitch. I barely knew the woman but the look on her face was enough for me to keep my distance. I knew she was toying with me. I was just too stubborn to ignore the bait.

"You wanna dance?" I asked Jeff.

"Lead the way." He smiled and in another life it may have made me swoon. However, tonight was not the night to think about what 'could be'. It was about letting my hair down and having fun. I was determined to enjoy my night.

I slipped my hand into Jeff's and we walked through the dense bar to the dance floor. Jeff's arm came around my waist and I wrapped my arms around his neck.

"You look stunning tonight," he complimented. It was genuine. Jeff was incapable of saying something like that with an agenda. He meant it. I was wearing a tight black dress that stopped mid thigh and dipped low to reveal my back. It clung to my breasts, exposing my cleavage, and showed off my curvy hips. I'd straightened my hair and let it hang down to the center of my spine.

"You look pretty sharp yourself, Stud."

He laughed and I enjoyed the rich sound. He did in fact look delicious in his dark jeans and black button down shirt. He was taller than most of the other guys here and to anyone who didn't know him, he would've looked intimidating. But I knew him and beneath that tough exterior was the heart of a man who deserved more than I could give. I touched the bruise on Jeff's face and he winced. "Does it hurt?" I asked, sincerely concerned. Jeff looked a little rough after Brody had punched him but he'd refused to let me come here alone.

"Not so bad," he replied.

"I'm sorry Brody hit you," I said, looking up into Jeff's green eyes.

His hand left my waist and he brushed my lips with his thumb. I held my breath and our gazes locked. "Don't apologize," his voice was husky, "if I'd had someone like you, and seen you with another man, I would've done the same thing. He still cares about you. I don't blame him."

I opened my mouth to say something but then snapped it shut again. I had no response to what he'd said and there was no way I was about to tell him I still cared about Brody too. I felt bad enough already, knowing that I couldn't return Jeff's feelings, no matter how badly I'd wished I could. A new, slower song started playing and I looked around the dance floor, my eyes fell on Brody and Sienna, dancing a few feet away from us. Their bodies were pressed up against each other and her height brought them almost nose-to-nose. She pressed her lips to his and I felt sick. I hated seeing them together but what right did I have to feel jealous? I had no claim to Brody and yet I felt fiercely possessive of him. Then there was the fact that I was ogling him while dancing with another man. God, what was wrong with me?

Jeff cleared his throat and I realized we'd stopped dancing. I looked up and found him regarding me. Guilt reared its head and the only way I could think of squashing it was to get another drink. Jeff and I made our way back to the table without exchanging a word or a glance and found Huntley and Grayson talking quietly between themselves. They looked so in love and if I hadn't adored them so much it would've been sickening to watch. Instead, I looked at them wistfully and wished that I had what they did.

A waitress stopped by and I ordered another drink, feeling the need to let go surfacing. I didn't want to think about anything tonight. I just wanted to let go for one night and *forget* that I was a complete mess inside. I found Brody and Sienna again, only this time Brody was watching *me.* His gaze was hot and determined and it angered me. The music had changed to a heavy RnB song and Sienna had made the most of the opportunity to bump and grind up against Brody, touching him in ways that could be considered public indecency. She obviously didn't notice him fucking me with his eyes.

I slammed another drink back, squeezing my eyes shut when my head started swimming. I'd started to go numb, my mind going blank. The glass the hit the table and everyone jumped, staring at me. I didn't care. Not right then anyway. *Mission accomplished,* I thought. I sent Brody a polite "fuck you" with my eyes, a message only he would be able to see, and spun on my heel before making way through the crowd to get to the bathroom. I waited in line and a few minutes later, someone grabbed my arm. "What the - "

My words disappeared when I looked up and saw that it

was Brody who'd grabbed my arm. He started dragging me further down the hall, past the men's bathroom and towards the storeroom. "What are you doing?" I asked, trying to pry my arm free. His grip was too strong and the alcohol I had consumed had made my ability to fight him weaken. He opened the door to the storeroom and dragged me behind him before shutting the door.

"Brody, what - " His lips crashed into mine before I could finish my sentence. They were hot and wet and so familiar. I pulled away, shaking my head. Those lips had been kissing another woman only minutes before and now he was kissing me? Yeah, I don't think - all coherent thought left my brain when Brody lifted me up and pushed my tight, black dress past my hips. He held my thighs and pressed his erection between my legs. He hadn't said a single word since he's dragged me into the smelly storeroom and while the lighting was bad, I could see his intentions written on his face. I'd lost my self-restraint about one minute ago and when he ground his erection against my wet thong a second time, I surrendered. Our lips collided in a heated, passionate kiss and his hands moved up while mine pushed through his hair. There was no other sound aside from our heavy breathing and it had a heady affect on me. My blood boiled and I was so turned on it was painful. I heard the rip of my underwear, the pull of a zipper and the tearing of a condom wrapper. Brody lifted me higher and started sucking on my neck as he pushed his hard cock into me. I bit my lip to stop from screaming out and gasped audibly when he was buried inside me to the hilt. It had been a year since I'd last had sex and while it took me a moment to adjust to Brody's size, I reveled in the way he filled me up, the way we fitted each other so perfectly you'd think we were made for each other.

Brody sighed, and bit my neck as his hips started moving. I

held on tighter and he started pumping into me until the sound of skin slapping on skin filled the room. It wasn't making love. It was fucking. Hot, uninhibited, forget-your-own-name *fucking.* It had been so long since we'd been like this but before I could overanalyze it, my orgasm attacked without warning. Brody kissed me, suppressing my scream and pushed into me hard and fast while he chased his own orgasm. When he grunted and shook in my arms, my head collapsed on his shoulders. My chest heaved and I fought to catch my breath. Brody's head came up and he looked at me, not saying anything. My post-orgasm bliss was cut short when an uneasy feeling settled over me. Brody lowered me to the floor, still remaining silent, and I righted my dress. He pulled off the condom, rolled it up in some toilet paper from one of the shelves, and tucked it into his pocket. He leaned in close and instead of kissing me on the lips he pressed a kiss to my forehead. I swear I heard him murmur "I'll always be yours" but I couldn't be sure because just as quickly as he'd fucked me into oblivion, he'd left and shut the door, leaving me alone. What the hell had just happened and why had I done that? I didn't just fuck people in storerooms. But then again, it wasn't just a person. It was Brody. I swallowed the bile rising in my throat and realized that I'd behaved like a total whore. Even worse, Brody had treated me that way, like I was a meaningless screw, while he was with someone else. *Oh God, what have I done?* I needed to get away. Now.

I opened the storeroom door and checked the hallway before making a hasty exit. I couldn't see Body, so I snuck out and walked into the ladies bathroom to clean myself up. When I caught sight of myself in the mirror, I was embarrassed. My hair was a mess, my eyes glassy and my cheeks red. That's when I started to feel sick for the second time in one night and it had nothing to do with the alcohol. It was caused by the hard reality that Brody had just screwed me in the storeroom like a dirty little secret. Somehow he'd managed to cheapen it and made me feel like trash. My eyes welled up and I wanted nothing more than to go home and take hot shower to wash Brody off of my skin. I cupped my mouth, choking back the urge to sob. I was being ridiculous and once again it proved that I was indeed a mess. The bathroom door opened and I was relieved to see Huntley walk in, concern written all over her angelic features. She looked stunning in her red wrap dress, her hair tied up with a few loose curls hanging free. Her blue eyes were darkened with worry and her mouth was set in a hard line.

"Demi, what's wrong?" she asked, taking a step closer.

"I – I – I don't know what just happened. I'm such an idiot. I don't know how it happened."

Her brows furrowed in confusion. "How what happened?"

"Brody, he just…we just… I didn't mean to but it just happened." I started crying harder and Huntley wrapped her arms around my shoulders. "You have to tell me what's wrong, Demi, so I can help you." She couldn't help me. I had to help myself.

"Brody took me to the storeroom and we…" I hesitated, fighting my urge to throw up.

"You had sex," Huntley said, finishing my sentence. I was glad that I didn't have to say it but somehow hearing it from her made it so much worse.

I nodded, mumbling, "I'm such a fool."

Huntley sighed and our eyes met in the mirror. Mine were red and puffy, while hers were clear and strong. I need that, more than anything.

"No," she replied, "you're not. You have a history with him and considering everything you went through with the baby. I'm surprised you've managed to keep it together this long."

"I can't go through this with him again," I cried, "Losing

him was hard enough the first time and now he has me tied up in knots. I don't know whether I'm coming or going when I'm around him and I hate that he still has so much power over me."

"You love him," Huntley stated, "and that will never change, especially after what you've lost in the process."

Before I could respond, the bathroom door opened and Sienna walked in. Her eyes darted between me and Huntley and her lips curled into a leer. I swallowed hard, feeling uncomfortable. The look in her eyes unsettled me.

"Let's go," Huntley said. I nodded and walked out, hearing Sienna's snicker disappear with the closing of the door.

I stopped in my tracks and Huntley came to halt beside me.

"Oh God," I whispered, "Do you think she heard us?"

"I doubt it, and if she did, she'd know better than to say anything to Brody."

As we headed back to rejoin the rest of our friends, I couldn't help the worry that took root in my belly. If Sienna had heard us, it would mean I'd have to tell Brody what happened when he left much sooner than I'd expected. And I just wasn't ready. I wasn't sure I'd ever be ready.

chapter thirteen

BRODY

I walked back to our table as if I hadn't just fucked Demi like a two-dollar hooker in the storeroom of Nicky's Bar. I was agitated as fuck and now I felt like an absolute asshole. I shouldn't have done that and somehow I'd managed to cheapen what Demi and I had and would always have. She was here with Jeff, but I couldn't resist the animalistic urge deep inside me to claim her, mark her with my body and remind her that she would always belong to me. I'd left Sienna at our table, told her I had to take a piss, and grabbed Demi while she was the line for the restroom. She was surprised, and maybe even a little pissed with me, but she hadn't stopped me. Not once. Instead, her tight little body welcomed me, reminding me just how tempestuous and combustible the chemistry was between us. She was still brewing after our argument last night, that much was obvious, but she did nothing to hide the desire her body felt for mine. It had been a year since we'd last had sex and it was still the most amazing sex I'd ever experienced. Only now I'd somehow tainted it by treating her like the trash I knew she wasn't.

It was supposed to be a fun night, a last hoorah for Grayson and Huntley before they got married in two days, but it had somehow turned into a wicked game between Demi and I. I was very aware that she'd been watching me all night and I did nothing to hide the fact that I was doing the same. It had soured my already bad mood, not only watching her with Jeff but also watching her attempt at getting drunk. My ogling caught Sienna's attention more than once but I didn't care. Only now, she was trying my patience and I hadn't had very much to begin with.

"I'm bored," she whined when she arrived back at our table. "When can we ditch this shithole?"

I glared at her and tried to get the tick in my jaw under control. "Feel free to leave, Sienna, but I'm not going anywhere. I'm here for my best friends, and if you'd rather not be selfless enough to suck it up for one night then call a cab."

She scowled at me. "I can't believe you'd put your friends above your girlfriend. I'm miserable and you don't seem to care at all."

I turned to face her and got in her personal space. "Let's be clear," I gritted my teeth, "you are not my girlfriend, and they're not just my friends, they're my family. If you can't handle them being such a big part of my life and the maybe it's time we re-evaluate this thing," I gestured between us, "with you and me."

Sienna straightened her back and her eyes hardened before she replied, "I'd be careful if I were you, Brody. You can lose everything in Chicago with one phone call to my daddy, so choose your moves wisely. I say when we're over, baby."

"Don't threaten me," I warned. "It won't end well. You wouldn't want your dear old 'daddy' to know you've fucked half of the board members and threatened them with that information. Extortion is a dangerous game, *baby,* especially when you have no fucking idea what you're doing."

We stared at each other. It felt like I'd come face-to-face with my biggest mistake and the phrase *"hindsight is 20/20"* popped into my head. I should've seen this coming because I knew Sienna was a manipulative, vindictive bitch, but I was hurting so badly at the time that we'd met that I hadn't stopped to think it through. Getting involved with my boss's daughter was probably the second dumbest thing I'd ever done. The first was leaving.

"I'm leaving," Sienna bit out. "I hope you will have changed your mind by the time you get back to the hotel. I'll be ready and waiting for you in bed."

She kissed me fast and hard but I held back. After what happened with Demi and I in the storeroom, it felt wrong to kiss Sienna back. I watched Sienna walk away and cursed under my breath. She thought I was going to have sex with her when I got back to the hotel. No way. For the first time the thought repulsed me. I didn't want to lay a hand on her. I was ruined all over again after being inside Demi.

Someone tapped me on the shoulder and I spun around. It was Grayson.

"Everything okay?" he asked.

"Yeah," I lied, "all good. What's up?"

'Huntley isn't feeling well, so I'm taking her home. Jeff is catching a ride home with us."

"What about Demi?" I asked, thinking about her immediately.

Grayson sighed and brushed his fingers through his hair.

"We're having a slight," he hesitated, "problem."

"What's wrong?"

"Demi is outside, but we can't let her drive home. She's had too much to drink. She's not too happy with us."

I'd seen Demi a little over thirty minutes ago. How much more could she have possibly had to drink? I followed Grayson outside to the parking lot where Demi was stumbling all over the place trying to get her keys out of Huntley's grasp. Jeff was leaning against Grayson's truck and he looked completely dejected.

"Shit!" Huntley cursed loudly.

My head whipped around and I caught sight of Huntley bending down to help Demi off the ground. She'd fallen onto the gravel and scraped her knee. Something about it amused her though. The alcohol must've numbed any hurt she might've felt. Jesus, how much had she had to drink? I raced over, and took her from Huntley's arms. I could feel Jeff's eyes on the back of my head but I ignored it. I had more important shit to deal with.

"Give me her keys," I said to Huntley. "I'll take her home and come fetch her car tomorrow."

Huntley looked worried but handed the keys to Demi's Lexus to me. "Are you okay to drive?"

"Yes," I replied, "I haven't had a drop of alcohol. I promise, nothing will happen to her. Don't you trust me?"

Huntley looked at a semi-conscious Demi tucked into my side and the back at me. The words that came next shouldn't have surprised me, but they did. They knocked me off kilter. "No, Brody, I don't."

Huntley kissed Demi's forehead and made her way to Grayson's truck. Grayson helped me get Demi into my truck and I watched the drive away before taking Demi home. It was silent in the cab of my truck. Demi was leaning against the window, her eyes closed.

"Why are you helping me?" she mumbled.

"Because you're too drunk to help yourself," I replied angrily. She had been completely irresponsible and it wasn't like her to get drunk, let alone consider driving home in her condition. What was going on with her? Was it my fault she'd had the need to get drunk off her ass? She didn't speak again until I stopped outside her house and walked around the passenger side to help her out.

"Don't touch me," she slurred, barely making it out the truck on her own.

"Stop being so Goddamn stubborn and let me help you," I bit back. I shut the truck door and picked her up, cradling her against my chest. "Did you enjoy it?" Her words were muffled against my shirt and I wasn't sure I'd heard her correctly. "Enjoy what?" I asked. I managed to unlock her front door without dropping her and walked inside. It was dark, save for the moonlight cascading through the glass doors that lead to her porch. A puppy started yapping, and Demi squirmed out of my arms. Her legs buckled beneath her but I grabbed her waist before she hit the floor. "Sshh, Coco," she hushed, making a grab for the little ball moving around our feet. "Go sleep." The puppy whined and traipsed off to its bed in the living room."You can leave now," Demi said, dismissing me. "I can manage without you."

Her words wounded me and I suspected that she'd meant them to, like what she really meant was that for the last year, she'd been managing just fine without me. I didn't want that to be true, but it was unfair of me to expect her to have spent the time wishing I hadn't left.

"I'm taking you to bed," I replied, helping her down the hallway to what I thought was her bedroom.

She laughed, but the sound was empty and cruel. "You

already did that once tonight, what makes you think I'll let you fuck me like a whore again?"

I winced. I couldn't deny that I'd acted like a complete asshole and now hearing Demi say that I'd done that to her made it so much worse.

"Do you fuck Sienna like that too? Or did you save it for me? Your piece of ass from home." She laughed again as I sat her down on her bed and I hated myself more than I ever thought possible. I found the switch for the lamp next to Demi's bed and turned it on just in time to see her fall backwards onto the bed. I bent down and slipped her heels off, trying not think about all the times we'd had sex while she was wearing nothing but those heels.

"I miss you," she whispered. My head shot up but her eyes were closed and I swore she'd fallen asleep. I stood up and helped her sit up right so that I could take off her dress. I unzipped it and slid it down over her shoulders to her waist. I laid her down again and continued sliding the dress down, over her hips and down her legs. She was wearing nothing but her bra, since I'd ripped off her underwear earlier, and I'm sure that if she weren't drunk she would have tried to cover herself up. Instead of leaving her like that, I opened her drawers until I found her pajamas and dressed her in her favorite lime green sleep shorts and matching tank top. I shifted her so that her head rested on her pillow and just as I was about to pull her duvet over her, her eyes flew open. Their lucidity, despite her state of intoxication, pierced my soul and left me bare for the world to see.

"I wish I could hate you," she said quietly. "But even with a broken heart, I still love you."

She climbed under her duvet and turned away from me, her breathing evening out as she fell asleep. I bent down and kissed her head, whispering, "I love you. Always."

I stared at her for a few minutes, struck speechless by her words, and rubbed my face. She was a mess, that much was obvious, and it was my fault. I turned to switch the light off when my eyes fell to a folded piece of paper. I picked it up and opened it. It took me a minute to figure out what it was. An ultrasound. Of a baby. What the fuck? Was she pregnant? I swallowed hard, feeling my body stiffen in shock. It wasn't mine so that meant it was...Jeff's. Demi had lied to me. Not only was she seeing Jeff but she might have been carrying his child. I felt sick. I dropped the photo and left. Nothing hurt more than thinking about her having another man's baby. It should be my baby she's carrying.

When I reached my truck, I took a few deep breaths but they didn't alleviate the pain coursing through every fiber in my body. Instead, I reared my fist back and punched the driver's side window of my truck. I watched the glass shatter and blood start running down my hand. It wasn't enough though. I deserved much worse. Then again, it couldn't get any worse than finding out the love of your life was expecting a child that wasn't yours.

chapter fourteen

DEMI

I woke up when my head started pounding. My eyelids were too heavy and it felt like I'd swallowed a box of lit cigarettes. A throat cleared and my bed dipped. With great difficulty, I cracked an eye open and found Huntley sitting next to me.

"What time is it?" I asked. I winced when my voice was unrecognizable, even to my own ears.

"A little after eleven," she replied. "How are you feeling?"

I groaned and lifted up onto my elbows, my brows furrowing when I noticed my state of semi-undress. I was wearing my sleep shorts and tank top, and had no recollection of how I'd gotten that way. I started looking around frantically, wondering if I'd come home with someone last night. Huntley saw the horror in my eyes and calmed me with a hand on my shoulder.

"Relax," she said quietly, "No one else is here." She leaned over and took a glass of orange juice and some Tylenol from the nightstand. "Drink this, you'll feel better."

I murmured "thank you" and swallowed the orange juice and Tylenol in one gulp.

Huntley watched me and I noticed her demeanor was more subdued than normal. I leaned back against my headboard. "Are you okay?" I asked.

She hesitated and then replied, "I'll run your shower, and then we'll talk, okay?"

She stood up but I grabbed her arm and stopped her. "What's wrong? Is this about last night?" I remembered bits and pieces about the night before but the details were still a little fuzzy.

Huntley sat back down next to me, and I saw her eyes had grown wet.

"You're starting to freak me out," I said, my throat growing thick with concern.

"I have something tell you." She swiped a tear that fell down her cheek and looked up to meet my worried gaze.

"Spit it out girly, I can't read your mind."

"I... I..." she paused and took a moment to compose herself, "This is harder than I thought it would be."

She needed some time and I'd give it to her. So I waited, and when she was ready to tell me what made her heart so heavy, I'd listen.

"I'm...I'm...I'm pregnant." She burst into tears and I had no idea what to say. The feelings running through me were nothing short of a *clusterfuck*.

"That's amazing!" I said. My enthusiasm was fake and I prayed that she couldn't hear it in my voice. I chalked it down to a killer hangover and nothing more, despite the menacing feeling unraveling in the pit of my heart and soul. I couldn't fall apart over this. Not in front of Huntley. "Why are you crying? You're supposed to be happy!"

"I am," she cried, her face red and puffy, "but I was so terrified to tell you."

"Why?"

"B-because I don't want you to hate me!"

I stared at my best friend, watching the way her lip trembled. She had been too afraid to share her news with me out of fear that I'd hate her. I could never hate her. I loved her too much.

I scooted closer and took hold of her shaking hand. "I could never hate you," I swallowed the emotion in my throat, "and I'm sorry that you were too afraid to share this with me. I'm happy for you Huntley, I really am. Does Grayson know?"

She shook her head. "No, I only saw the doctor yesterday to confirm it. I wanted *you* to be the first to know."

I squeezed her hand. "How far along are you?"

She gave me a genuine half-smile. "Only ten weeks."

"I'm sure Grayson will be thrilled."

"I know he will," she laughed lightly. "He wanted us to have another baby, little did we know I was already pregnant when we decided to start trying. I didn't think it would be so easy to fall pregnant a second time."

"It was meant to be," I whispered, feeling my own eyes burning. I wanted Huntley to think it was because I was happy for her, but it was really because a small part of me died inside. Did that make me a bad friend? Probably.

Huntley wiped her face and gave me a hug. *Keep it together,* I told myself.

"I love you, Demi, so much. You're my best friend."

"I know," I replied quietly, trying not to allow my emotions to get the better of me, "I love you too."

We pulled away and Huntley looked at me sheepishly. "Are you okay after last night?" she asked. It was my turn to look sheepish.

"I don't know," I replied, "I don't remember much. Care to fill me in?"

"You had a little too much to drink," she explained. "And Brody had to drive you home."

My brows furrowed in confusion. "Brody?"

Huntley nodded and I saw the same question in her eyes that was burning itself into my mind: Why would he do that? *Because he still cares.*

Thinking about him triggered memories about the night before and as they flashed in my mind, my body went rigid and my eyes widened. The night started off drama-free for the most part and ended with...*Brody and I...having sex...in the storeroom.*

"What is it?" Huntley asked. I'd obviously done a bad job of hiding my shock.

I shook my head, plastering on a fake smile. "It's nothing. I'm fine."

"Are you sure?"

"Yes. It's all fine."

I could tell she didn't believe me but it wasn't in her to push for information.

"Okay," she acquiesced, standing up with a heavy sigh. "I have to leave, but I'll see you at the rehearsal dinner tonight?"

I nodded. "Yeah, I'll see you there."

Huntley was half way out the door when she stopped and turned to face me. "Are you sure you're okay?"

"I'm fine," I lied. "Promise."

She disappeared out the door and I heard the front door shut a few minutes later. I sagged against my headboard and I knew I was holding on by a thread. It was all too much to deal with at once. I threw the covers off and padded my way across my soft plush carpet into the bathroom. I stared at myself in the mirror and chocked back a sob when I didn't recognize the woman staring back at me. It had been a while since I'd felt like that and it all started when Brody showed up.

I turned my shower on and waited for the water to reach scalding hot before stepping in. The hot water soothed my aching muscles but my heart still hung heavy in my chest. I was a mess and I'd only made it worse for myself by allowing Brody to fuck me like a whore in a storeroom of a bar. "Oh God," I cried out, finally letting the dam break. I slid down the wet tiles and hugged my legs, resting my forehead on my knees. Guilt had made itself at home in my blood and pumped through my veins. Huntley and Grayson were expecting their second baby and I couldn't even muster enough selflessness to be completely happy for them. I wanted so badly to be excited for them. But I wasn't and I'd openly lied to my best friend about how her news really made me feel. I felt cheated, because I had so much taken from me. I felt guilty because I would have never begrudged Huntley and Grayson their happiness. I felt broken because everything had fallen apart all over again in a matter of days. I felt alone because I'd lost everything that I'd dreamed of having. Including myself. I had no idea where to go from here. Except, I had no choice but to move forward and get through it, just like I did before. This was what life was about wasn't it? Rising above adversity and beating the odds. I'd done it once, so I could do it again. Couldn't I?

My body shook with every sob and I cried until there was nothing left. When it was all over I wasn't sure if I had it in me to pull myself out of this hole. Until I remembered the last words Brody had whispered to me after he'd put me to bed last night.

"I love you. Always."

chapter fifteen

BRODY

I sipped my whiskey and closed my eyes to savor the burn as it traveled down my throat. I was brooding, replaying the night before in my mind over and over again until I'd convinced myself it really happened. My night had not ended well and the darkness I felt lurking inside me hadn't left. Sienna was angry as all hell when I arrived back at the hotel, but I'd ignored her and decided I'd rather sit in the bar until dawn than deal with her hissy fit.

"Hey man." Grayson greeted me and took a seat at my side. We were sitting inside Aunt Emma's bakery, which had been elegantly decorated for Huntley and Grayson's rehearsal dinner. The lighting was dimmed and waiters walked around offering appetizers until the main course was ready to be served. It was a small space, but with the open windows that overlooked the street and the romantic decor and lighting, it was perfect and so Huntley and Grayson.

"Hey," I replied, looking into the bottom of my whiskey tumbler. If I looked at Grayson he'd just ask too many questions and I was in no frame of mind to answer them. I was still trying to put it all in perspective and it wasn't going well.

"What happened to your hand?" Grayson asked, eyeing the bandage.

"Got hurt," I replied. "It's nothing." I wasn't about to tell him that I'd punched my trucks' window in or why. The thought crossed my mind that Grayson might've known about Demi's pregnancy, but I didn't think he'd keep something like that from me. Grayson started saying something but it fell on deaf ears as the object of my wayward thoughts walked in through the door. Demi was wearing a one-sleeved emerald cocktail dress that looked stunning against her creamy skin. She wore her favorite black peep toe wedge heels and they made her legs go on for miles. Her beautiful red hair was pinned to one side, luscious curls hanging over her shoulder and covering her breast. She was every single one of my wet dreams come to life and seeing her felt like a stab to the lungs - excruciatingly painful.

"What's up with you tonight?" Grayson asked.

"Nothing," I grumbled, my eyes never leaving Demi. Grayson followed my gaze. "Man, you two need to stop dancing around each other and get your shit together," he said quietly. I could hear the exasperation in his voice.

"It's not that simple," I replied.

"Because of Sienna?" *No. Because the woman I'm in love with, and have always been in love with, is pregnant with your brother's child.* The words got caught in my throat so I just shook my head in response. As devastated as I was, I couldn't tell Grayson anything. I had no idea if anyone else knew but it wasn't my news to share. *But it could've been,* my inner voice taunted truthfully.

"It just is," I said quietly. I watched as Demi greeted Huntley and her family, and then moved on to Grayson's family. I froze when she hugged Jeff, searching for any sign that he knew, but came up empty when their embrace was a little too cold for a couple who was expecting. Unless he had no idea.

I groaned, feeling more and more infuriated with the mess I'd found myself in.

"Look, I'm here if you need to talk," Grayson said, patting my back. "I hate seeing you like this."

Shame filled my body and it took a lot not to hang my head. My best friend was celebrating his upcoming wedding and I was acting like a complete jerk. This wasn't about me and yet I was making about me.

"I'm sorry, Gray. It's been a rough few days. I'll pull my head out of my ass long enough to celebrate with you tonight."

He laughed and rubbed the back of his neck. "I know, Brody. We've had more drama in three days than on a soap opera. It's ridiculous," he paused, "which is why I need to ask you something." He looked up and grinned like the lovesick fool he was when he found Huntley dancing in the middle of the room with Hunter on her hip. She too looked stunning, and I couldn't have chosen a better person for Grayson to share his life with.

"Shoot."

He hesitated for a second and looked up at me. "Why are you with Sienna?"

His question didn't surprise me, but I decided that of all the people in my life, he deserved the truth, especially since I'd been behaving like a total douchebag.

"Honestly? I don't know. In the beginning it was a way for me to get my mind off things. I tried to keep it casual, but the next thing I knew I was being dragged to dinners with Sienna's father. I should've known getting into bed with my boss's daughter was the worst idea ever."

"It's none of my business, but she's not the right woman for you."

"Oh yeah? Then who is?" I asked somewhat playfully. He turned his head and motioned towards Demi. She was dancing with Jeff on the makeshift dance floor and when she threw her head back in laughter, a sickening knot formed in my stomach from knowing that I should have been the one holding her, making her laugh.

"Things are a mess between you two," Grayson added, his tone sad, "but I think you need to talk. There are a lot of things that were left unsaid after you were gone and Demi went through a really rough time - "

"What do you mean?" I interrupted, "I thought she got over it?"

Grayson frowned and he almost looked angry. "Who told you that?"

I shrugged. "I just sort of assumed, since I hadn't heard from her again."

"You have it all wrong, man, and I'm so tempted to tell you everything but I can't. I won't get in the middle of this again. I will, however, say this, if you truly believe you and Demi can't fix this mess you've made, then get on that plane in two days and don't look back. Leave her behind. But if you think there's a chance, no matter how small, that you'd be willing to lay it all out there again, just to be with her, then put all the other bullshit aside and begin again. Start over."

I thought about the sonogram picture I'd found and the reality of it all hit me harder than a six ton wrecking ball. Even if I wanted to try fix my relationship with Demi, it was obvious she'd moved on. It was a realization that I had to make peace with, no matter how hard or how shattering it was.

"It's a little more complicated than that. It's out of my control now, and that's something I have to deal with."

"Your choice," Grayson said, "but for the record, I think you're making a mistake."

He stood up and left me alone with my self-deprecating thoughts. I wanted nothing more than to leave but I couldn't, or wouldn't, do that to Huntley and Grayson.

I stood up and walked towards the restrooms. I needed to freshen up a little and pull my shit together long enough to get through tonight and tomorrow, then I'd be on a plane out of here and never look back. It was time for me to move on, something I thought I'd already done, but after the past few days I'd realized that all I'd managed to do was bury it all deep enough so that it wouldn't see the light of day. As I passed the lady's restroom, I overheard voices. It sounded like Huntley and Demi. I squeezed my eyes shut and told myself to keep walking, but my feet had other ideas. Against my better judgment, I leaned in closer to the door that sat slightly ajar and listened.

Huntley spoke first. "But you have to tell Brody before he leaves. Don't you think he deserves to know?"

I heard a sniffle and assumed it was Demi. "I'm not ready to tell him yet."

There was a moment of silence before Huntley replied, "If Jeff knows about the baby, don't you think you owe it to Brody to tell him too? You can't keep…" her words disappeared when I heard the words "Jeff' and "baby". My ears started ringing and my throat grew dry. So it was true. Demi was expecting Jeff's baby. Oh fuck, I was going to be sick. Bile slid up my throat and I barely made it to the bathroom before I spewed all the contents in my stomach into the toilet bowl. It was final. I'd lost Demi for good and that wasn't even the worst part. What killed me, what slaughtered my soul, was knowing that another man was going to get *my* dream. He was going to have a family with Demi, something I'd dreamed about for most of my grown up life. It was over for me. There was no coming back after this and the only person I could really blame was myself. I rinsed my mouth and washed my face before making my way back out just in time for the speeches to start. I reluctantly took a seat next to Sienna and had to contain my anger when I saw Demi and Huntley walk out shortly after me. Demi sat down next to Jeff and I had the sudden compulsion to fly across the table and beat the shit out of Jeff for taking what was mine. It was irrational and I knew that. Another man can't take what you think is yours when you so freely gave it up. It was my biggest fucking mistake ever.

Coach Morgan, Huntley's uncle stood up and the room quieted. We were seated at a long rectangular table and it worked well. The rehearsal dinner was for family and close friends and I suddenly regretted having Sienna with me.

"Good evening everyone," Coach Morgan started. "Emma and I would like to thank you all for being here tonight, it means a lot to us. Firstly, to my beautiful niece, Huntley, baby girl, your parents would be so proud of you and I know your aunt and I couldn't be more proud of you than we are right now," there were a few sniffles from the woman and I looked to where Grayson had his arm wrapped around an emotional Huntley. "We want you to be happy, sweetheart, and we love you like a daughter. Grayson," Coach Morgan looked at Grayson, "I don't think there is a better man out there to take care of our girl and I believe my brother hand picked you from above to take care of Huntley. My wish for you both is a life of happiness and love, the kind that lasts a lifetime. Be good to each other."

There was a collective "cheers" and "hear hear" from

everyone and smiles all round. The moment Sienna stood up, I knew the magic of the night was about to be shot to hell.

"Excuse me, everyone," Sienna said, earning a few glares from the other guests. "But I have an announcement. Well *we* have an announcement," she looked at me and the words that came out of her mouth left me speechless. It was like watching a car crash in slow motion and I could do nothing to stop it. "Brody and I are expecting."

What.The.Fuck.

The silence in the room was cut short with gasps from all around the table, mine included. Sienna smiled, despite the obvious tension that her announcement had caused, and looked straight at Demi. Her face was pale and utterly crestfallen.

She rose from her chair and walked to where Sienna was sitting. Her hand came up and she slapped Sienna across the face. Hard. Sienna cupped her face, looking surprised. Hell, even I was surprised. Demi wasn't the type to hit anyone.

"You bitch," she said. "Are you so desperate for attention that you'd try and ruin my best friends rehearsal dinner? You should be ashamed of yourself!" Her voice cracked and when her eyes fell on me I could see the hurt swirling in their depths. Without another word, she walked past me and Sienna and broke out into a run the closer she got to the door. Huntley followed and I could only watch in embarrassment as it had all unfolded. Grayson glared at me and he looked beyond pissed. I couldn't blame him. Sienna grabbed my hand and it was the first time I'd looked at her all night. I was such a fucking moron for getting involved with her and now I was tethered to her in the worst way.

"Aren't you going to say something?" she asked. She's put her 'sweet' mask on for me, but it was too late. I'd already seen the monster she was beneath the façade and I didn't like it. Grayson flew out of his chair and stomped towards the exit.

"We'll talk about this later," I growled at Sienna.

"So typical!" she shrieked, throwing her hands up in the air. Causing a scene was her specialty and it was sickening that she got her kicks out of it. She had no idea how badly she'd just fucked things up. "I just told you we're pregnant and your response is to run after your poor, pathetic ex-girlfriend!"

I took her arm in my hands and pulled her close enough that she could be the only one to hear me talk. "It's time for you to leave, Sienna. We'll talk about this back at the hotel, but right now I need to check on my friends."

I left her there and walked outside into the warm night. I found Grayson and Huntley standing on the sidewalk but no Demi.

"Where is she?" I asked.

Huntley's hand came up and connected with my cheek, making my skin sting.

"You asshole!" she yelled between her tears.

"What the hell, Huntley? What did *I* do?"

"Baby," Grayson soothed. "Please calm down."

'No, Gray, I've had enough of all of this. Our night has been ruined because if *his,"* she pointed at me, "bitch of a girlfriend!"

"I'm sorry," I said. "I had no idea that was going to happen. Now, tell me where I can find Demi, please."

Huntley shook her head. "No, you've done enough. She was fine until you showed up. I love you Brody, and your one of our best friends, but right now I don't like you. Demi deserved better. She's been through hell and back again because of you!"

"Huntley," Grayson warned with a shake of his head, "Don't."

They seemed to be having a silent conversation that I clearly wasn't privy to.

"I'm sorry," I apologized again. "I know I've fucked up real bad, but I need to talk to her Huntley."

"I'm also sorry, Brody, but I don't think it's a good idea. She needs time, and she needs the chance to really get over you. I want you at our wedding tomorrow, but Sienna isn't welcome and if she shows up I won't hesitate to have her thrown out."

I rubbed the back of my neck and looked away feeling contrite.

I started to speak but Grayson cut me off. "Why don't you go inside, baby?" he said to Huntley. He was worried about her. Even I noticed the change in her behavior. Huntley wasn't always so verbal about her feelings, let alone her anger towards someone. She nodded and Grayson kissed her forehead before she disappeared inside again.

"Listen, Gray - "

"No, Brody, *you* listen. You are my best friend and God knows I love you like a brother, but enough is enough. I'm going to tell you something and you won't like it, but I'm the only one will give it to you straight. It has taken almost a Goddamn *year* for Demi to be anything like herself again. I know I said it isn't my story to tell, and it isn't, but you need to understand what it did to her when you left. I hate seeing you two do this to yourselves and each other, and now you've got a baby on the way with Sienna. I..." he paused, and rubbed his face with both his hands, "Fuck. I don't know what to say anymore."

I sighed and stuck my hands in the pockets of my jeans. "Man, I've fucked things up so badly I don't know which was is up. I don't know where to go from here."

"Be honest with yourself for one thing. You know in your heart what the right thing to do is. No one can you fix this, except you." He patted me on the back. "I'd better get back in there. I'll catch you later."

I watched him walk away and allowed his words to sink in.

I knew what I had to do. I just needed the courage to do it.

****

When I arrived back at the hotel, Sienna was sitting on the king size bed waiting for me. I'd decided to walk back and used the time to think about what I had to do.

"I was wondering when you were going to come back," Sienna said as she sauntered towards me. She was wearing a silk nightgown and was most likely naked underneath. Looking at her now, I asked myself, not for the first time, why I'd gotten involved with someone like her. What attracted me to her?

"I had to apologize for the scene you caused," I replied quietly, my voice calm. She rolled her eyes and put her hands on my chest. I clutched her wrists to stop her from moving her hands further down. She was trying to seduce me and after her performance at the bakery there was nothing about her that turned me on anymore. "Don't be so dramatic," she said. "I thought you'd be happy."

I started thinking about it and couldn't understand how she'd gotten pregnant in the first place. We'd never had unprotected sex. I was more than cautious about suiting up when I had sex with her. Demi was the only woman I'd ever not worn protection with and I was determined to keep it that way. Sex with Sienna was just that. Sex. But with Demi it was always *more.*

"Tell me how," I said. "We've never had unprotected sex, Sienna."

She snatched her hands away and tried to look hurt. "You're doubting me?"

"Yes."

"I didn't sleep around, if that's what you're insinuating."

"You're lying, Sienna, but we're going to deal with it when

I'm back in Chicago."

She frowned. "What do you mean?"

The hotel phone rang and I answered. "Hello?"

The concierge's voice came through the phone. "Good evening Mr Scott. I called to let you know that the town car is ready to take you to the airport."

"Thank you. We'll be right down."

I put the phone down and said, "Pack your bags. The town car is here to take you to the airport."

"What?"

"I took the liberty of booking you a flight home while I was walking back here. Your flight is in a few hours but you can't stay here."

"You can't do that," she almost yelled, her face contorting into a scowl. God, did this woman ever smile?

"I can and I did. Now, I'm going to shower, and when I come out you'd better be gone."

I didn't give her a chance to reply. I pushed past her, pulling off my clothes one item and at a time, and locked myself in the bathroom. I stood under the hot spray of water and felt a new form of determination settle in my gut. I had to fix this mess, even if it meant I came out the other end without Demi. It was time I got my life in order and it started with coming home. For good.

chapter sixteen

HUNTLEY

I stood in front of the full-length mirror in my aunt and uncle's bedroom and stared at the woman in front of me. It was my wedding day, a day I'd been waiting for, for what felt like forever. There was a light knock at the door and I smiled and said, "Come in."

I saw Demi's reflection in the mirror as she slipped through the door and her face broke into a broad smile. "You look…breathtaking, Huntley. The most beautiful bride I've ever seen."

"Thank you," I reply, returning her smile. I look myself over one last time. My dress was truly a work of art, made from lace and lace applique with a romantic silhouette that featured capped sleeves and v-shaped neckline. My hair was curled, then twisted and pinned into a low side ponytail with pin curls resting on top of it. A beautiful crystal embellished tiara rested atop my head and held my scalloped fingertip veil in place. With light pink blush, peach gloss and thick lashes, I looked elegant and it was everything I had dreamed it would be.

I turned around and faced Demi. She too looked incredible in her full-length strapless, one shoulder gown, Champaign in color. It was ruched across the breasts and accented by a black band around the waist with a diamante flower detail on the side. I'd had it made especially for her. Her make up was also simple, but where I had light pink plush, the apples of her cheeks were more peach and her lips had a nude gloss. I watched her warily, wondering what kind of toll the night before had taken on her. She hid her feelings well, but the sadness in her eyes were unmistakable.

"Are you almost ready to go?" she asked, walking closer.

I nodded and asked, "How are you?"

"I'm fine," she replied quietly. "I don't want you worrying about me today. It's *your* day."

I pulled her into a hug and felt my throat constrict. She backed away when I sniffled. "Don't you dare cry. You're going to ruin your make up!"

I giggled and replied, "Sorry. I'm all over the place. I've been waiting for this day for so long, it still doesn't seem real."

Demi smiled. "Oh it's real, and we'd better get going before we're late. Grayson won't be impressed."

I thought about my husband-to-be and my heart soared. I'd missed him last night. He'd spent the night at his parents' house, and while we both protested it in the beginning, we didn't want to break tradition and start our marriage off on the wrong foot.

There was another knock at the door and my aunt Emma stepped in, looking regal in her caramel colored pleated chiffon gown. "We're ready to go, sweetheart. It's time."

Demi and I grabbed our clutch purses and followed my aunt outside to the car. When we stopped outside the gates of Lake Dixon nerves unraveled in my stomach and when I saw how beautiful everything looked I couldn't help but gasp. There were three marquee tents set up, all over looking the lake. The one to the far left was our makeshift chapel with chairs on each side of a white isle covered in red roses. The two marquee tents, a little way down, were slightly bigger and had wooden flooring. From where I sat in the car, I could see round tables that surrounded a dance floor and a few tables that were set up for the buffet dinner. My uncle Alex stopped outside another much smaller tent and as soon as I stepped outside, I was hustled inside and away from curious eyes of our seated guests.

"You look beautiful sweetheart," my uncle said, smiling.

"Thank you," I replied. "And thank you for agreeing to give me away today. It means so much to me." I swallowed the emotion in my throat, wishing so much that my mother and father could be here. They'd missed all the big moments - Hunter's birth, and now my wedding - and their absence today was sorely felt.

'I'm honored that you've given me the privilege, sweetheart. I know I'm not your dad, but I love you and I want this day to be a dream come true. I've said it a thousand times already, but your Aunt Em and I are so incredibly proud of the woman you have become."

I nodded, unable to form words and hugged my uncle around the waist. He wasn't my father, but I wouldn't have had anyone else give me away. He'd earned the privilege when he had so graciously welcomed me into both his family and his heart. I loved him dearly for that.

"Places everyone," my aunt announced. She walked up to me and handed me my bouquet of white and roses. "You ready?" she asked.

"Yes, I'm ready."

I slipped my hand into the crook of my uncle's arm and took a deep calming breath. We walked outside, the late afternoon sun shining around us, and my uncle led me to the entrance of our chapel tent. Hannah and Finley, looking adorable in their champagne colored flower girl dresses, skipped their way down the isle, and then Demi followed with Jeff at her side. I took a minute to savor this moment and when I looked up, Grayson found me.

GRAYSON

My breathing hitched when my eyes collided with Huntley's as she made her way down the isle. She was a vision in her wedding gown, with her hair swept to the side, and even through her veil I could see her smile. My heart raced and I felt moisture building in my eyes. Jeff reached over and squeezed my shoulder. "You okay?" he whispered.

I grinned. 'I've never been better."

As I stared at my beautiful bride, all the other guests disappeared and all that was left was her and me. We'd been through hell and back to get here and I wasn't going to take a single second of it for granted.

They reached the makeshift alter and Coach Morgan lifted Huntley's veil, placing a gentle kiss in her cheek. I saw his eyes grow a little wet as he went to stand next to his wife. I took Huntley's shaking hand in mine and gave it a reassuring squeeze. I mouthed, "I love you" and her returning gaze was filled with the love and adoration she held for me. I looked over my shoulder, checking to see that Hunter wasn't fussing with my mother, before giving my full attention to the priest.

"Who gives this woman away?" he asked.

Coach Morgan and his wife both said "we do" and I thought it was rather fitting. It was because of them that Huntley had turned out to be the incredible woman I saw standing in front of me. The priest told everyone to sit down and finally got on with the show. I was grateful for the short ceremony and almost jumped with excitement when it was time for the vows. My eyes never wavered from Huntley's as she repeated the priest's words.

"I Huntley Morgan, take you Grayson Carter to be my husband, to share the good times and hard times side by side. I humbly give you my hand and my heart as a sanctuary of warmth and peace, and pledge my faith and love to you. Just as this circle is without end, my love for you is eternal.

Just as it is made of incorruptible substance, my commitment to you will never fail. With this ring, I thee wed."

She slipped my platinum wedding band inscribed with our wedding date on my finger and then it was my turn.

"Huntley, as I stand here before you, my eyes looking so deeply into yours, I see all of the things I fell in love with and so much more. I stand here before you, my heart beating so loudly in my ears, and I find myself so lost for the right words to say. Standing here with this ring in my hand reminds me how you complete me, heart and soul. With every smile, every embrace, every tear you've ever wiped from my face, it reminds me how blessed I really am, how I can't ever thank the Lord above enough, for allowing you into my life.

It reminds me of every laugh we've ever shared, every hard time we made it through together, and every beautiful moment there is to come. I give you this ring, my heart, my soul. I give you everything I am today. I promise to love you, protect you, be with you forever, and cherish every moment as if it were the last moment on earth. I love you. With this ring, let it be known, that over every other person in the world I could be with, you were chosen for me. Let it be known, that with this ring, I'm promising to be here for you for all eternity, 'til death do us part."

Huntley sniffed and wiped her tears while I slipped her princess-cut diamond wedding ring onto her delicate finger.

"Ladies and gentleman," the priest continued, "it is a pleasure to present to you, Mr. and Mrs. Grayson Carter. You may kiss your bride."

I stepped closer to Huntley and cupped her face with my hands. "I love you, Mrs. Carter," I whispered. I pressed my lips to hers and her body immediately relaxed into mine. I deepened the kiss, earning a few whistles and hollers from the guests. When we pulled apart, Huntley's eyes were wet and bright, and the love I saw there mirrored my own.

"My husband," she whispered, "and father of two."

I frowned momentarily and then…

"What?"

"You heard me," she replied, more tears streaming down her face.

"You're…we're…"

"Yes," she cried, cupping her mouth.

"God, I love you." I picked her up and swung her around, feeling overwhelmed with love and pure happiness. I didn't care that we had audience because in my mind it was just us. Always me and her. When my lips met hers a second time and our bodies pressed together, peace settled over us and I knew it was the start of our forever.

chapter seventeen

DEMI

I sat at our table and watched people milling about, some dancing, some talking to other guests. We were under a beautifully decorated marquee tent next to Lake Dixon with the most exquisite sunset imaginable. As the last rays of sun flickered away and gave way to a starry night sky, tee lights in mason jars lit up and gave the whole atmosphere an ethereal feel. It was perfect for Huntley and Grayson's wedding, and everything I'd imagined it would be. I sipped my champagne and somehow managed to lose myself in the experience. I saw Huntley and Grayson dancing while Lifehouse's 'You and Me' drifted through the speakers. Like many of the other guests, they and the endless, perfect love they shared transfixed me.

A light tap on my shoulder broke my haze and I looked up to find Jeff smiling at me. He looked incredibly handsome in his classic black tuxedo and champagne colored vest. He'd removed his jacket and rolled up his sleeves, giving his debonair look a slightly rogue effect. It was sexy, and any other woman here would've buckled at the knees just looking at him. If only he'd had that effect on me. It would have been far easier. He was a safe choice for me. Too bad I was too stubborn to choose what was safe, instead of what ended up destroying me inside.

"Care to dance?" he asked, giving me his heart stopping lopsided grin. I smiled, and placed my hand in his, wanting to feel something other than the mess inside me. I'd spent the night before curled up in bed, crying until my eyes ached. But I didn't want to feel that tonight, and certainly not with Jeff.

"I'd love to," I replied. I finished the rest of my champagne and followed Jeff as he led me onto the dance floor. His right arm wrapped around my waist and his left hand held mine while I rested my free hand on his shoulder. We were pressed close; close enough for anyone to think we were actually a couple. I wished we could be. I wished that I could feel more for Jeff. But I couldn't.

Our bodies swayed to the music and I rested my head on his shoulder. For those few minutes I was able to forget what troubled me and simply allowed myself to just *be.* I focused on the steady rhythm of Jeff's heart and closed my eyes. I'd spent the night before curled up in bed, sobbing until my eyes ached.

"You're quiet tonight," Jeff said in low voice. I looked up and found him studying me.

'I'm fine," I replied. I plastered on the fake smile I'd been wearing all day in the hopes that he'd believe it.

"You want to talk about it?" he asked, concern furrowing his brow. "I know last night couldn't have been easy for you." He was referring to the news Sienna had decided to share in the middle of Huntley and Grayson's rehearsal dinner. The news that had unraveled all the progress I had made because it reopened a wound that would never be completely healed.

"Please," I sighed, "I don't want to talk about it. I just want to enjoy the rest of my night."

"Why won't you let me help you, Demi?"

"Because you can't. No one can."

He tilted my head up with his index finger and pierced me with his gaze. "You can't carry it all alone. Please, let me help you. Let me be there for you."

His words sunk in and when he lowered his head, brushing his lips across mine, I knew we were both having an entirely different conversation. He wasn't just asking me to let him help me. He was asking me to give myself to him. He didn't need to say the words. It was all there in his eyes.

"Jeff, I..." I struggled with the words, not only because I didn't know what to say, but also because I knew I was about to break his heart.

"Have you considered the possibility that it's time to move on?" he asked.

We stopped dancing and stood in the middle of the dance floor. "I have moved on," I said. It was a lie, but it was a necessary lie. I had to convince myself more than anyone else that I had actually moved on from Brody.

"Then prove it," Jeff challenged, "Move on...with *me*."

"I don't think – "

"I love you," he blurted out quickly, looking down at my face.

"I love you too," I replied. "You're one of my best friends."

"You're misunderstanding me," he leaned in, "I'm *in* love with you, Demi. I want you to be with me, as my girlfriend."

My hands dropped to my sides and I took a small step back. I'd known this moment was coming ever since Brody's grandmother had pointed out how Jeff really felt about me.

"I can't," was my only reply, and this time I wasn't lying to him.

"Why not?"

I swallowed hard. "I'm not the woman for you, Jeff."

"How can you decide that for me?"

"I love you, but not the way you want me to. I just don't see you that way. You're a good - "

"Don't say friend, please. I thought after some time you'd start to feel more, but maybe I misread all the signs."

"I didn't mean to lead you on. I'm sorry – " Jeff put his hands up and I stopped talking.

"I'm such an idiot," he mutters, looking defeated.

"I can't lose you," I choked out, "I still need you in my life, please."

Jeff shook his head. "I don't know if I can."

"Jeff, please," I pleaded.

"I need some time," he sighed. He pressed a chaste kiss to my forehead and walked away, leaving me standing alone. A hand came to rest on my forearm and I turned around to find Huntley.

"Is everything okay?" she asked. The look on her face closely resembled pity and I hated it, but I couldn't lie to her.

"No," I replied. "I can't be around both of them right now. It's just too hard. I'm sorry, but I think it's time I left and went home."

"I understand. Call me if you need me, okay?"

I nodded. "I will. I love you, and I'm so happy you and Grayson finally got your happy ending. You both deserve it." I blinked back my urge to cry, I'd been doing that way too often lately, and settled for hugging my best friend.

"You deserve it too," Huntley whispered.

"I want to believe that," I sighed, feeling drained. "But I just need some time."

Huntley pulled back and looked at me. "Everything will be okay, you have to know that Demi. You're strong enough to get through it."

I couldn't respond because I had a hard time believing things would ever be okay again. God, I hated myself for being so *weak*.

"I'll call you tomorrow," I said.

I walked towards our table and picked up my purse. I poured one last glass of champagne and before I could throw it all back at once, Brody snatched it out my hands.

"What are you doing?" I asked. Irritation flared and I had to stop myself from going off on him. Who the hell did he think he was?

"I could ask you the same thing," he replied. I noticed the tick in his jaw and the way he ground the words out. He was mad. I just couldn't understand why. We'd barely glanced at each other all day.

I threw my hands up in exasperation. "What ever," I muttered. "I'm tired and I'm going home." I turned my back on him and headed towards the exit of the marquee tent. I heard Brody following me but I didn't care. I pulled my keys from my purse and walked through the other cars until I found mine. I opened my door and then Brody slammed it shut.

'You're not driving," he said, sounding angrier than before. My irritation morphed into rage.

"The hell I'm not," I snapped, trying to open my car door.

"You've had too much to drink, and you're obviously upset. You shouldn't be driving in your," he hesitated, "condition."

I scowled at him. 'What the hell are you talking about my 'condition'?"

"Just give me your Goddamn keys, Demetria, or we'll be here all night."

I was too tired to fight so I threw my keys at him. They hit his hard chest and bounced onto the ground.

"Fine."

I walked around to the other side and climbed in, making sure to slam the door. If he insisted on treating me like a child then I'd behave like one. He slid into the driver's seat, looking hot and disheveled in his black tuxedo. His hair stood in all directions, probably from running his fingers through it more than a few times, and his face was hard. He was quite a sight, even when he was pissed off.

We drove through the gates and onto the road, the silence stretching between us and growing more intense. I wasn't going to speak first. I had nothing I wanted to say to him.

He muttered something under his breath and turned my face to glare at him.

"What was that?" I asked.

"Nothing," he grunted.

"If you have something to say, Brody, then just say it! I'm so sick of your stupid games!"

"This isn't a game, Demetria." He drove faster and if I hadn't trusted him so implicitly, I would have been scared. We reached the edge of town and I was relived to almost be home. I needed to get away from Brody, and fast. He was no longer good for me, I realized.

"Well then grow a pair," I said, "and tell me why you felt the need to drive me home when I'm perfectly capable of taking care of myself. I've been doing it for the last year and I sure as hell won't stop when you leave again."

"For fuck's sake," Brody half yelled. He pulled to a stop outside my house and I didn't bother waiting for whatever explanation he'd come up with. I ran up the stairs and unlocked my front door before hurriedly entering. Again, Brody was hot on my heels.

"I know you're no longer the same person you were, Demetria, and neither am I, but I didn't realize you'd become so irresponsible."

I whirled around and faced him, unable to keep a lid on my brewing indignation. "What are you talking about, Brody? You keep talking in circles, so just spit it out!"

"You were drinking, and last I heard that's not good for the baby."

His words caught me off guard and I froze, feeling the color drain from my face.

"What baby?"

"The one you're carrying, Goddamit! And don't lie to me. I saw the ultrasound!"

I was so confused. "What ultrasound?" My voice shook.

"The one next to your bed, I saw it when I brought you home the other night."

Oh God. No no no no. How could I have been so reckless?

"It's not – "

"Don't lie to me, not about this. You said you weren't seeing Jeff, which was obviously a lie too."

"No, I wasn't lying. There was nothing going on between us."

"Are you telling me you're pregnant with *someone else's* baby?" The disgust in Brody's voice was thick and protruding. I stared at him, until finally I couldn't take it anymore. I cracked.

"NO!" I bawled, feeling hot tears spill over my eyelids. "It was *our* baby! That ultrasound is of YOUR baby!" I placed my hand over my mouth and cried, watching Brody's face blanch. My secret was out, and there was no way for me to take it back, no matter how hard I wished for it. I clutched my stomach, fighting the need to double over. I closed my eyes and immediately regretted it…

"Can someone help us, please?" Huntley asked, looking around at the Emergency Room nurses. It was three a.m. and I'd called Huntley after I woke up bleeding. I knew something was wrong. I could feel it.

The truth was, as surprised as I was about my pregnancy, I was excited. It had been a difficult few weeks but I'd focused on the little life in my belly and it had somehow given me something other than Brody to live for. He'd left me two months ago, and yet the ache in my chest hurt as if it was yesterday that he'd walked out my front door. I hadn't spoken to him at all, and when he did call, I ignored it. If he knew about the baby he would have stayed because he had to and I wasn't prepared to carry that on my shoulders. So instead, I'd lost one thing and gained another. A part of me wished he was here to experience this with me but I silenced it when I reminded myself that our life together wasn't enough for him. I doubted having this baby would have made him want *to stay.*

"What seems to be the problem?" and elderly nursed asked, looking at us from over her glasses.

"My friend is pregnant and she's in a lot of pain and she's bleeding."

The nurse walked around the counter and her eyes grew wide when she saw me. I was pale and when I looked down, I saw blood trailing down my leg.

"Who's your doctor?"

"Dr. Bates," Huntley replied quickly. I was in too much pain and too scared to say anything. I was losing my baby.

The nurse hurried to the phone and after a quick phone call, she came rushing towards us with a wheelchair. I sat down, crying out in pain, and I was wheeled to the Maternity floor where we found Dr. Bates waiting for us. Without saying I word, he escorted us into a delivery room. Nurses started hooking me up to all kinds of equipment and I started panicking. Dr. Bates pressed my hard belly and I cried out.

"We're going to do an ultrasound," he said. The expression on his face was of no comfort and only added to my distress. A nurse squirted

a cold gel onto my skin and Dr. Bates wasted no time. He pressed the wand onto my belly and moved it around.

"Dammit," he muttered. He turned to face me, looking forlorn. "Miss. Rosemead, I'm sorry to have to tell you this but I can't find a heartbeat."

The floor dropped from beneath my feet and once again my world came crumbling down.

"W-why?" I asked, "What's wrong."

"I'm afraid you have a case of placental abruption, and if we don't deliver your baby now, you could bleed out." He didn't give me time to respond before a nurse separated my legs and removed my panties. My dress was lifted up to my waist and I leaned up on my elbows to see what he was doing.

"She's already dilated, and we don't have time for a C-section," he said to a nurse. He turned his gaze back to me. "You have to deliver your baby naturally Miss. Rosemead, but you're too far dilated for an epidural - "

"Is the baby okay?" I asked, cutting him off. When he didn't answer immediately, I yelled, "Tell me!"

"No," he paused, "I'm afraid your baby has died."

I stared at him and felt the life drain from my own body. My baby was dead. It couldn't be. It had to have been a nightmare and I would wake up any second. It wasn't real.

"Oh God," Huntley cried next to me. I looked up at her and burst into tears. My baby. Dead.

I screamed when a sharp pain shot through my abdomen.

"Doctor," a nurse said, "We're ready."

He nodded, and took a seat at the end of the bed between my legs.

"Okay, Miss. Rosemead, I'm going to need you to push. Now."

"No," I cried. "Please, it hurts too much."

Huntley squeezed my hand reassuringly but it didn't help. I was devastated, and now I had to deliver my dead baby.

"Push," Dr. Bates ordered. I shook my head, and cried harder.

"Please, no. I can't do this. I can't."

Huntley cried next to me and I realized that while it was a nightmare, it was in fact real, and I wasn't going to wake up.

"Please push Demi, you have to do this," Huntley pleaded with a tear streaked face. I took a shaky breath and started pushing. The pain was excruciating and it felt like I was being sliced through the middle. Dr. Bates ordered me to stop but the reprieve didn't last.

"Please," I sobbed, "make it stop."

"We're almost there, Miss. Rosemead. Push."

I gritted my teeth and bore down, giving it my all. It wasn't until I saw Dr. Bates lift the baby that it all really sunk in. When a nurse took the baby from him, I waited for the cry. It never came.

"What is it?" I asked.

Dr. Bates looked up from where he was cleaning me up, sadness marring his face. "A girl."

"A girl," I whispered. A little girl.

She was wrapped in a pink blanket when they handed her to me and for a short time I had no idea what to do or say.

"Did you have a name?" I looked up at Huntley and then back down at my daughter.

"Gracie," I replied, struggling to get the word past the lump in my throat. "Her name is Gracie."

Her eyes were closed, but I imagined they were brown like Brody's. She had a sprinkling of hair on her head, light and blonde. At only five months she was already her daddy's girl. Only that wasn't true, because she was gone. With teary eyes I pressed a kiss to her forehead in the hopes that she knew she was loved, no matter how short her time on Earth had been. She was made up of the best parts of me and Brody, something I would always remember. I suddenly felt exhausted. So very tired. I couldn't understand why my heart was still beating, and my little girl's wasn't. It was cruel.

My eyes started to flutter shut my limbs started going numb. I whispered a 'good-bye', because really, that was all I had left to give, and the last thing I remembered was Dr. Bates yelling, "Miss. Rosemead, stay with me!" Everything went dark after that, and I felt nothing. I was consumed by a darkness that never ended.

****

It was A few hours later when I started regaining consciousness. The harsh light above me hurt my tired eyes and I cowered away from it. My head was in a hazy fog and I fought it.

"Demi?"

I opened my eyes slowly, and saw that Huntley was standing above me, her face still red.

"What happened?" I croaked, rolling to my side to face her.

She sniffled and I saw relief flood her stormy blue eyes. "You passed out because of the amount of blood you lost, sweety. They had to do a blood transfusion. It was touch and go there for a while."

"And the baby?"

Huntley looked down and started crying again. "She's gone."

"So it really happened?" I asked, feeling the onslaught of tears coming again. Huntley nodded and in that moment, it felt like the fight had left my body.

Huntley crawled in next to me and wrapped her slender arms around my shaking body. She carried the weight of my loss with me, and in some ways it helped lighten the burden. I found myself stuck in the darkness again, only this time I saw no way out. There was no light left. It was just an abyss of endless…black.

chapter eighteen

Brody

Demi crumpled to the floor in a sobbing mess and it took every bit of inner strength not to go to her. The need to comfort her came as naturally to me as breathing, but I'd decided that just this once depriving myself of that was the right thing to do.

"*My* baby?" I asked, my voice barely audible. Her head hung low but she still nodded. I fisted my hair and inhaled deeply. It was all I could do not to fall to floor myself. I looked around the dark house and tried to wrap my head around Demi's admission. I thought back to all the times I'd seen her this week, remembering that I hadn't once seen her with a baby. She cried harder and I took a step closer. A brown puppy was pawing at Demi's legs, but even then Demi remained on the floor while her body shook. Her broken cries taunted my ears and as much as I wanted to pick her up and hold her to me, I wasn't going to.

"Where is it?" My tone came out harder than I intended. "The baby, I mean."

When Demi finally looked up at me, I saw the light leave her eyes and it made me afraid of the answer. I could tell it wasn't going to be good. "Tell me, Demetria," I pressed.

"She died," Demi whispered. Time stopped just then, and I felt the air leave my own lungs. *She?*

"We had a daughter?" I swallowed and felt my eyes grow wet. When Demi didn't say anything more I fell to my knees in front of her and gripped her forearms. "Why didn't you tell me?" I yelled. Tears started sliding down my face but I didn't care. I'd just been sucker punched and betrayed by the woman I've loved more than life itself since I was six years old. I think I deserved to fucking cry. Demi flinched, and looked away.

"Why didn't you tell me?" I yelled again, "I deserved to know!"

"Brody," she cried, "I'm s-sorry. Y-you w-would have s-stayed for t-the wrong reasons if I had told you. I c-couldn't keep you here, so I l-let you go!"

A sense of loss overcame me and collided with the anger and duplicity coursing through every fiber in my body. My blood boiled with it, my bones ached with it.

"I can't believe you would hide this from me," I said. Looking at her felt like looking at a complete stranger. I didn't know her, not anymore, and that hurt me almost more than learning about our child.

She shook her head and I loosened my grip on her arms, still afraid that I'd hurt her. I was pissed, but I wasn't about to hurt her physically.

"I t-tried to t-tell you," she sobbed.

"When? I never heard from you!"

"I w-went to Chicago two months after she..." Demi

swallowed, struggling with the words, "died, but I saw you with Sienna and thought you had moved on."

I sat back and wiped my face. The gravity of the situation hit me square in the chest. It wasn't only her fault. If I hadn't left none of this would have happened.

"How did she die?"

"Oh God, Brody, please, I can't take anymore right now!"

"Do Huntley and Grayson know?"

Instead of replying, Demi just curled further into herself and I realized that I wasn't going to get the answers I wanted.

"If you can't tell me, I'll find someone who will," I said standing up. Before I left, I turned around and looked at her one last time.

"I felt like shit for months after what I did. I was consumed with my guilt for months. Now, I find out you kept our child and her death from me! You are no better than I am, and *you* have to live with this. There's no coming back from this, and this time it's on you."

I slammed the door shut, drowning out her cries, and walked with determination to her red Lexus. There was no way in hell I was going anywhere until I had some answers.

****

I pulled up the hand break and the car screeched to a halt on the dusty gravel of the parking lot next to Lake Dixon. There were fewer cars now, but when I spotted Grayson's truck, I knew he was still here. The fact that it was his wedding didn't stop me. Nothing would.

I found him standing on the side, talking to Huntley, Jeff, his parents, Coach Morgan and his wife. They all laughed, and smiled, but when Grayson spotted me his smile fell.

"Brody, what's wrong?" he asked, right before I knocked

him on his ass. I ignored the pain, since I'd hit him with injured hand. It didn't compare to what I was feeling inside.

"What the fuck?" Jeff yelled, moving to pin my arms behind me. Huntley bent down and helped Grayson to his feet while everyone glared at me.

"You sonofabitch! How could you not tell me?"

"Tell you wha - " Grayson snapped his mouth shut and I saw realization flicker across his face. I would apologize for hitting him later, when I wasn't so angry.

"She told you," he said quietly, barely above a whisper.

Everyone went quiet, and their expressions morphed from shock to a combination of sheepishness and sympathy…

"You all knew, didn't you?"

No one replied and they could barely look me in the eye.

"Fuck," I muttered, pulling away from Jeff. "Is this some kind of sick joke?"

"No," Huntley replied. She opened her mouth to say something more but I cut her off.

"I called you," I looked at Grayson, "every day for three fucking months, and you didn't think to mention any of this to me?"

"It's not that simple," he replied.

"Why not?" I shouted. "You're my best friend, and you betrayed me! Every fucking one of you betrayed me!"

"Demi wanted to be the one to tell you," Jeff said from behind me. I spun around to face him, itching to hit him too.

"And how would *you* of all people know that?" I snapped, stepping closer. Coach Morgan and Grayson's father, Richard, also take a step forward, flanking Jeff on either side. I didn't care. I would punch all of them if I had to.

"She flew to Chicago to see you, but she saw you with someone else."

I snorted. "So that's when you decided to swoop in and

rescue her, right?"

He inched closer until we were toe-to-toe. He was only an inch taller than I was, so I'd have no problem taking him. The fact that we'd been friends for most of our lives didn't seem to matter to either of us.

"She was a mess because of you and she needed a friend. I won't apologize for being there for her when she needed me," he growled.

"Does she know you're in love with her?"

Jeff went quiet and looked down. I wasn't an idiot. A blind man could see he wanted to be more than just friends with Demi. He thought I hadn't seen them together on the dance floor earlier, or the way he'd stormed off. He was wrong. My eyes had been on Demi all night and my guess was the conversation hadn't gone the way he wanted it to.

"That's what I thought," I snarled.

"Will you stop?" Huntley said angrily. She stepped next to Jeff and fixed her glower on me. "Jeff was there for Demi when she needed *you,* but you weren't there - "

"And whose fault is that?" I threw my arms in the air. "You can't blame me if I had no idea what the fuck was going on."

"She did it for you," Huntley said. Her face fell slightly and I saw sadness in the depths of her eyes. "You wanted to leave, so she let you go."

Huntley's words sunk in and my vexation gave way to the insurmountable sorrow that had settled in my chest. I was only now starting to see the aftermath of my decision to chase after more than what I had, when the truth was, I had everything I wanted right in front of me. I grabbed the nearest chair and sat down, resting my head in my hands. "She couldn't even tell me what happened," I said softly, struggling with my own emotions. I couldn't tell which way was up.

Huntley and Grayson exchanged a few words, and then

she was gone. Grayson took a seat next to me and sighed deeply before turning his gaze my way.

"Look man, I'm sorry I didn't tell you, but Demi asked me not to and it wasn't my secret to tell. I feel like shit for keeping it from you, I really do, but Huntley and I had a hard enough time keeping Demi together as it was."

I contemplated pressing him for more answers and as enraged and anguished as I was, I needed to hear them. It was my own form of torture, knowing how destroyed Demi was, knowing how much she'd gone through while I was gone. I knew I wasn't entirely to blame but I still carried the responsibility of throwing away more than I could've imagined.

"I need you to tell me what happened," I said, finally looking at Grayson.

"Shit," Grayson muttered, pulling his fingers through his hair, "I don't know if I can."

"Please," I begged, "You owe me that much."

"I guess you're right," he paused, and then continued, "but are you sure you want to this now? Here?"

I nodded, preparing myself for only God knows what.

"From what Huntley told me, Demi was twelve weeks along when you left. She was excited, and scared, but asked us not to tell you because she wanted to be the one to do it. One night, Demi called us, and looking at Huntley's face I knew it wasn't good. Huntley said Demi was in a lot of pain, and she was bleeding a lot, so Huntley took her to the hospital. She was only twenty weeks along at that stage so we were all worried." Grayson stopped for a second and I could tell he was struggling, obviously trying to figure out how to tell me the rest. "Demi was rushed into the delivery room and the Doctor said she had what they call a Placental Abruption. I don't know specifics but apparently it could be fatal to the mother, but when they did the ultrasound, they saw that the baby had already died. Demi had no choice but to deliver the baby naturally, and afterwards," he swallowed hard, his voice thick with emotion, "she almost bled out. She was in the hospital for a few days, and then she had to go for grief counseling. They had her strung on all kinds of pills to help her with depression and not sleeping. She stopped eating too, until Huntley made her realize that we didn't want to lose her too - " when Grayson saw me face, he stopped midsentence. He remained quiet and simply put his arms around my shoulders. My body shook and I didn't care if people saw. I was a grown man, crying like a baby, because of what the woman I loved had endured. Alone. I felt like a coward, and more importantly like I'd failed Demi, and our child. I had nothing left of myself to give, so I gave in. I surrendered to the desolation that had annihilated my heart and soul. Was I being punished for leaving Demi in the first place? I didn't know. All I knew was that I could feel my heart breaking, feeling every piece slip away until there was nothing. In the end, I walked away from everything I'd ever wanted, and now I would never get it back. That last thought took what little fight I had left in me, leaving me bereft. I had no idea what to do, except weep. So I did.

chapter nineteen

HUNTLEY

My aunt Emma and I stopped outside of Demi's house and I raced up the stairs, wedding gown and all. As soon as I saw Brody walk into the marquee tent with the murderous, tear stained expression on his face, something deep down stirred and I knew why he'd come back to the wedding. He was right though, we had betrayed him, but we had to respect Demi's wishes at the time. I realized after seeing Brody's reaction that it was wrong to keep something so important from him and there was absolutely no excuse for it.

I knocked on Demi's door, and grew more frantic when there was no answer. I grabbed the handle and then saw that the door was unlocked. I pushed it open and stuck my head in. When I saw Demi hunched over on the floor, I immediately walked towards her and bent down at her side.

She was crying, and chanting "I'm sorry" and "she died" between her hiccups.

"Demi?"

Her head flew up and she looked dazed, like she was looking right through me. It took her a few seconds to focus and realize that it was me I front of her. She threw her arms around me and cried into my neck.

'I'm sorry, I tried to be strong but I couldn't anymore."

"It's okay girly, I'm here now. Everything is going to be okay," I replied softly, rubbing up and down her back. I hated seeing her like this. It only reminded me how fragile she still was, and how hard it had been for her to pretend that everything was fine when it wasn't. Part of me felt responsible because we 'hovered' constantly, asking if she was okay instead of allowing her to take the time she needed to deal with cards life had handed her.

My aunt appeared at the doorway and looked at the two of us with a sympathy-filled gaze. "What can I do?" she asked me. Demi's puppy, Coco, was lying next to her and rested her head at Demi's feet.

"Would you mind feeding Coco?" I asked. "I'm going to try and get Demi to bed."

My aunt, the amazing woman that she was, nodded and quietly picked the brown Labrador up before disappearing into the kitchen. I helped Demi to her feet and get her to her bedroom. It was late, just after midnight, and I was tired after a long yet perfect day, but my best friend needed me and I wasn't going to let her down, married or not.

I sat her down on her bed and waited for her to catch her breath. She was distraught and I wondered what had happened between her and Brody.

When Demi was calmer, and her breathing was back to normal, I took a chance and asked, "You want to tell me what happened?"

She sniffed. "Brody found one my old sonogram pictures and thought I was pregnant with Jeff's baby."

I frowned. "Why would he think that?"

Demi shrugged, looking completely defeated. "He thinks there was something going on between us, even after I told him Jeff and I are just friends."

"I guess you finally told him about the baby." It was a statement, and I just needed to confirm it for myself.

Her head bobbed up and down. "It was awful. I made a huge mistake by not telling him sooner, I see that now, but I was so scared he'd stay and end up being miserable. I couldn't do that to him. It wasn't fair."

That was Demi, always thinking about others before herself. It was one of many things that endeared me to her so completely.

"He'll come around," I said, "He just needs some time."

Worry creased her brow. "Did you see him?"

"Yeah," I sighed, "he came back to the wedding and found Grayson. They're talking right now. He's a mess."

"Oh God," Demi breathed, "What have I done?"

I wrapped my arms around her shoulders and squeezed. "You did what you thought was best for you and your child."

"No," she retorted with her a shake of her head, "I ran. I should've told him, Huntley. He deserved to know, and now I'm scared it's too late. I can't help but feel like this is really the end, and I don't know how to let go of him. He's my true love, my soul mate, and my other half. I've lost him for good this time. I can feel it."

I couldn't tell her she was wrong, because it wouldn't have been true, and I wasn't about to give her false hope. But what I could do is support her, just like I had before, and help her get through this.

"What you need to focus on right now is *you,* and believe that everything else will work itself out. Just give it some time. I also think it might be a good time to go see Dr. Hansen again. I'd hate for this to derail all the progress you've made."

"I will," she replied softly. Her eyes met mine and I understood, better than most people, the kind of despair they reflected back at me. I'd been there more than once and I chose to believe that Demi would get out of it. She just needed to keep hanging on to the bit of the light that had broken through her darkest days.

"Thank you for being here," she said, "and I'm sorry you had to come on your wedding night. This is my mess, and it's time I take ownership for my actions."

I waved her off. "I would have been pissed if you hadn't told me, so it's a good thing Brody showed up and punched Grayson."

"He did what?"

"He knocked Grayson flat on his ass."

Demi's eyes started misting over again. "Oh my, I'm so sorry!"

"Hey," I looked her in the eye, "it wasn't your fault. He was angry, and to be honest I couldn't really blame him. I actually felt sorry for him."

"I think I broke his heart," Demi whimpered. I didn't know what more to say. Working through her guilt and everything else she was feeling wasn't something I could do for her. It was something only she could get herself through.

We sat in silence for a while until my aunt walked in. "I made you some tea," she told Demi.

"Thank you."

Demi placed the hot mug on her bedside table and I could see just how tired she was.

"Do you want me to stay with you tonight?" I asked her.

"Don't be silly," she replied, looking at me like I'd lost my mind, "You just got married. There's no way you're spending your wedding night with me when you should be with your husband."

"Are you sure?" I asked.

"Yes, I'll be fine. Promise."

"You'll call me if you need anything right?"

"I won't need to," she replied, stifling a yawn.

I stood up and took out a fresh pair of pajamas for Demi to wear to bed. I also took out some of the prescribed medication Demi's therapist prescribed when she wasn't sleeping. I handed them to her and made sure she took them. I knew she wouldn't be sleeping otherwise. She was exhausted so I stayed long enough to make sure she got into bed and fell asleep. Most friends wouldn't have done that, but Demi was more than my friend. She was my sister. She'd seen me through some of my darkest days and Hell would freeze over before I abandoned her when she needed me.

chapter twenty

BRODY

I breathed my first sigh of relief when the plane touched down at O'Hare International airport. The last twenty-four hours had been more than I could handle and sometimes didn't even feel like they really happened. I was overwhelmed with a tirade of conflicting emotions and felt weighed down. After I'd spoken to Grayson, I decided to catch the first flight back to Chicago so that I could make sense of what was going on in my life, my head and my heart.

I walked to the luggage carousel with determination and despite my emotional exhaustion I knew I had a few things to take care of while I was here. My phone rang and when I saw Sienna's name flashing on the screen I pressed 'ignore'. I'd see her later at my apartment and what we needed to talk about couldn't be said on the phone. I thought about Demi but pushed the thoughts aside quickly. I couldn't deal with her. Not yet.

I hailed a cab and in the short time it took for us to arrive at my apartment building, I'd never felt more out of place until then. I thought the city was my home but it couldn't have been further from that. It was cold and clinical to me now, lacking the effervescence that only Breckinridge could provide. I told myself it was Breckinridge itself that made it *home,* but that too was a lie. *Demi* was my home, and it saddened me that I'd lost sight of that.

I paid the cabby and carried my bag upstairs. When I walked into my apartment, the lights were all on and some trashy reality television was playing on my flat screen. Sienna was here.

Good.

I could deal with her now rather than later. I told myself it was like ripping off a Band-Aid, but I knew it would be more like sawing off my leg with a butter knife. Not pretty. I dropped my bag on the floor and walked towards my bedroom, where I heard the shower going. I regretted giving Sienna a key to my place, but there was nothing I could do about it now. It wasn't going to be *my* place for much longer anyway.

I stood in front of my bedroom windows that overlooked the city skyline that had once captivated me. I used to be enthralled by it, drawn to it. But now it meant nothing to me. It only reminded me of a time in my life when I'd been nothing more than an immature *boy*. After the last few hours, I felt like I'd aged, and at some point I'd started looking at my life and my decisions with a different, more worldlier perspective.

My phone vibrated and this time it was Grayson. Sienna was still in the shower so I took the chance to talk to Grayson. He'd be my voice of reason while I mulled over everything swimming around in my head.

"Hey, man," I greeted.

"Hey man. Just checkin' in. Wanted to make sure you landed."

"Yeah," I replied. "I'm at my apartment right now."

"Sienna there?"

"She's in the shower."

There was silence on the other end of the line and it dawned on me that Grayson might have gotten the wrong idea.

"Alone," I added. "She was here when I arrived."

"I would ask you why she has a key to your apartment, but I'd rather not know. As long as you're not having second thoughts..." His words drifted and he allowed the incomplete sentence to hang in the air.

"Hell no!" I replied harshly, earning a chuckle on the other end. "It will take me some time to wrap shit up here, but there's no looking back now."

"Glad to hear it," Grayson said. I could practically *hear* his shit-eating grin on the other side. "Looking forward to having you back home, man. We can finally start working out the plans for the ranch."

"As soon as I have all my shit together here, I'll be on the first flight out. I just have a few things to take care of, you know."

"You know where to find me if you need help, bro. Just call."

"Yeah, man. Thanks." Just then Sienna's phone started ringing and I grabbed it from the bedside table, frowning when I didn't recognize the number. "Listen, I have to go, but we'll catch up again tomorrow," I told Grayson. He said goodbye and I immediately answered Sienna's phone.

"Hello?"

A woman's voice came through. "Good evening, I'm looking for Sienna Johnson."

"She's not available right now, but I'd be happy to take a

message."

The woman's voice became muffled and she said something to someone else in the background. I waited for a second before she spoke to me again. "I'm calling from the River North Fertility Clinic. I was hoping to confirm Miss. Johnson's appointment for tomorrow at ten a.m."

Fertility clinic? What?

"I'm sorry," I replied, "but you must be mistaken. Are you sure you've called the right Sienna Johnson?"

Something felt off and alarm bells starting going off in my head. Finding out that Sienna was supposedly pregnant had been a shock, and one of the reasons I'd wasted little time coming back to Chicago.

The woman hesitated, and I imagined she was checking the information they had on file. She then read Sienna's address through the phone and assured me she did in fact have the right person.

"Can you tell me what treatment she's coming in for?"

"I'm sorry sir, but I'm not allowed to disclose patient information unless it's a spouse."

"I'm her husband," I lied quickly, growing more and more unsettled with the conversation.

"That's strange, Miss. Johnson failed to mention a husband."

"We're newlyweds, she hasn't a chance to change any of her information yet." The lie fell from my lips easier than I felt comfortable with.

"It appears Miss Johnson has only made an initial consultation, after which we can determine her course of treatment," the woman said.

"So she's not pregnant?" I asked dubiously. I probably sounded like an idiot, judging by the woman's growing exasperation on the other end.

"No," she replied, "I'm guessing that's why she contacted us. Our patients are generally those who struggle to conceive."

I swallowed, and pinched the bridge of my nose. It was all starting to make sense to me now.

"Okay, thank you. I will be sure to relay the message."

I ended the call and sat down the bed. I heard the shower turn off - finally - and waited for Sienna to come out of the bathroom. She emerged a few minutes later, a towel that left much to be desired wrapped around her body and her head. She knew she was a gorgeous woman, and never hesitated to use it to her advantage. Unfortunately, I had been one of the stupid fools to fall victim to that.

"You're home early," she said in greeting. "I thought you would be a few more days." She dropped her towel and sauntered towards my closet in all her nude glory. Her lack of modesty came of no surprise, and yet it did nothing for me.

"I'm sorry to disappoint you," I replied, just as she reappeared wearing one of my shirts.

"I'm not disappointed." She made a move to climb onto my lap but I gently pushed her away. She scowled, and just like that the alluring seductress she wanted to be was gone.

"We need to talk."

Sienna huffed, and crossed her arms over her chest. "About what?"

"Your phone rang while you were in the shower," I said, rubbing my jean-clad thighs. "I answered it."

"Who was it?"

"River North Fertility Clinic."

Sienna's face dropped momentarily, and then the cold, calculating mask slipped carefully back into place.

"Why on Earth would they be calling me?"

I watched her carefully, my eyes scrutinizing her face first and then dropping down to her flat stomach. Not surprisingly, I wasn't thrilled to hear that she was pregnant, or that she chose Huntley and Grayson's rehearsal dinner to share the news. It was like her to do that kind of thing, make herself the center of attention when someone else was in the spotlight. Hearing that she'd lied had only shown me what kind of heartless, conniving person was hiding behind her perfect exterior. All I could say was she had some major issues and I was done dealing with them.

"They wanted to confirm your appointment for tomorrow morning," I said.

"I didn't make an appointment - "

"Stop lying," I snapped. I stood up and walked closer to her. "Just stop lying, and for once tell the truth! You're not pregnant, are you?"

"Brody, I can explain - "

"No, I'm done listening to your bullshit, Sienna. You lied to me, and you did it in front of my friends and family. I.Am.Done. Do you hear me? No more! Tell me why you did it?"

"I..." her mouth opened and closed before she grew completely silent. We both knew that I'd caught her, and that it was the final straw.

"I can't believe you'd go so far," I said, "but the really sad part is that you thought I'd ever want to have a family with you. Did you think I was so gullible to believe you?"

Sienna's eyes grew hard, and her spine straightened. She wasn't giving up that easily. It wasn't in her nature, not even when she knew she'd already lost.

"I knew what would happen when you saw your ex. You'd go right back to her and I wasn't willing to give you up without a fight."

"I'm not yours to fight for," I argued. "We aren't a couple!"

Sienna reared back as if I'd slapped her, and it crossed my

mind that she was a brilliant actress. We'd agreed from the beginning that this was nothing more than a relationship of convenience, nothing more than two people satisfying physical needs and temporarily filling a void that would have otherwise stayed empty. Somewhere along the way though, something changed, and I'd obviously been too busy to notice. Or maybe I simply chose not to notice.

"I can't believe you!" she shrieked. A saw a tear slip down her cheek and I waited for the pang of guilt or remorse to hit. It didn't. Sienna was just playing the game, even though I was throwing in the proverbial towel. If I was going to get my life back on track, I had to start somewhere.

"Believe me, sweetheart. It's over."

"Then so is your job," she replied looking smug. This wasn't the first time she'd threatened me. I knew as well as she did that fraternizing amongst co-workers was strictly against company policy, so our relationship remained somewhat of a secret. I think her father had his suspicions, but if he did, he never mentioned it either.

"Doesn't matter. I've set up a meeting with your father tomorrow and I have my letter of resignation ready. I'll give my notice and be out by the end of the month."

"You're leaving?" Sienna sounded surprised. Ironic, considering she'd probably seen it coming.

I ignored her question. "I'm going to head out for a while. I think it will be best if you're gone by the time I get back."

Without giving her time to respond, I walked back into my living room and it dawned on me just how suddenly out of place I felt. I didn't belong here, and I was starting to realize I never had. That was the beauty of hindsight. It smacked you upside the head when it was almost too late to right your wrongs. I tucked my hands into my pockets and decided to walk to the bar a few blocks away. I could use a drink…or six.

****

When I arrived back at my apartment a few hours later, it was well close to midnight and I was glad to find it empty. I didn't bother switching the lights on as I took out a bottle of whiskey and sat down on my sofa. I poured some of the amber liquid into a tumbler, not bothering with ice, and took a large gulp, savoring the burn. Something in me toyed with the desire to call Demi, but I fought it tooth and nail. It was too soon. I had too much to work through before I considered speaking to her again. I needed to forgive myself for the mistakes I made a year ago, and then I could work on forgiving Demi for keeping such a life changing secret from me. I needed time to grieve a loss I'd only just experienced, even if it happened eight months ago, and then I needed a plan. Either way, Demi was part of that plan, and in the end, I couldn't picture my life, present or future, without her.

chapter twenty-one

DEMI

I walked into Dr. Hansen's office, and she smiled at me from behind her large Mahogany desk. She was a beautiful woman with honey blonde hair tied up in a bun at the base of her neck. Behind the dark from her glasses sat light blue eyes that were as kind as they were stern. She might not have known it, but I owed her my life.

"Demi, please, come in. Make yourself comfortable."

It had been two months since Huntley and Grayson's wedding, and two months since I'd seen or heard from Brody. After everything that happened the last time I saw him, I'd decided it was time to take back control of my life, and my emotions. That's why I'd been back to Dr. Hansen. She was the psychologist I started seeing after the grief of losing the baby became too much, and I wasn't afraid to admit that I needed her help again. For the last three weeks I'd been seeing her twice a week. Until now we'd almost skirted around that last day I had with Brody but I had a feeling I'd be facing it today.

"So, how are you?" Dr. Hansen asked. She took a seat on the sofa opposite me and started writing on her notepad. I often joked that she could write an entire book based on the notes she'd made during my previous sessions, but she reassured me that there was always someone else going through something much worse. It was her way of saying that feeling sorry for myself wouldn't benefit me. So I'd listened.

"I'm okay," I replied, "just tired."

"Have you been sleeping?" she asked, not looking up yet.

"Not much. I've been trying to sleep without using any medication, but its difficult. I can't sleep without dreaming about…"

"Brody," she finished for me. "And your baby."

I nodded my head and swallowed. "Yes."

Dr. Hansen looked up and met my apprehensive gaze. She knew this was hard for me to talk about, but she'd keep pushing until I'd laid it all out there. I hated it, and it tore me up every time, but I knew that it was a necessary evil.

"Have you thought about the possibility that your dreams are your subconscious' way of saying that you haven't been able to truly let go of your trauma and forgive Brody for what he did?"

"I don't know," I replied honestly. "I thought I'd let it go but then Brody showed up and I was knocked right back to square one."

"Have you spoken to Brody since you told him about the baby?" Dr. Hansen asked, scribbling more notes. I fiddled with my fingers in my lap.

"No."

"Don't you think it's time you did?"

I sighed. "I don't know. I'm scared to speak to him, I guess."

Dr. Hansen looked up at me again and I knew I wasn't going like what she was going to say.

"It will making moving on with your life harder if you don't talk to him. You need closure, something you didn't have before because until now, Brody hasn't really featured. I want you to ask yourself, and you don't have to answer me right away. Have you forgiven him for what he did?"

I knew the answer, so I replied, "I know I haven't, but I also feel guilty because it wasn't entirely his fault that I was alone when the baby died. He chose to leave, but I chose to keep it from him."

"That's a very accurate and mature observation, Demi. I also want you to think about this: how can you forgive him when you haven't forgiven yourself? Your baby's death wasn't your fault, and it wasn't Brody's. It was a very unfortunate turn of events that neither you or Brody could change, even if he hadn't left you."

I looked down at my intertwined fingers, unable to say anything for the moment. The truth was, I *did* blame myself for losing our baby. It's impossible to describe what it's like when you lose a child when you're a woman. Our bodies are made to bare children, grow them, and give them life. But for some reason I failed. Or at least it felt that way.

"Demi? Are you alright?"

I looked up at Dr. Hansen's concerned face and realized that I'd zoned out in the middle of our session.

"Yes, sorry," I replied. "What did you say?"

"I asked if you've taken the time to forgive yourself and considered taking the time to think about where you want to go from here?"

I looked out the window overlooking lush green grass, observing the way the sun seemed to brighten the world outside.

"I just want to be happy again," I replied simply. "I want to close my eyes at night and not worry about whether or not I'm going to have the same recurring nightmare again. I want to live my life without the weight of *everything* hanging over my head like a dark cloud."

"Does Brody feature into that?"

"I've thought about it, but I don't know how we can move forward after all of this *stuff*. I'd be surprised if he ever spoke to me again, if I'm being honest."

Dr. Hansen put her notepad down and moved to the end of the sofa. She took my hand in hers and gave it a squeeze.

"I think the real question here is what do you want going forward? If it's being happy, then work on finding what makes you happy again. And if Brody features into that, then let it be."

"I'm scared," I admitted almost sheepishly. "What if he doesn't forgive me?"

Dr. Hansen smiled. It was warm and reassuring. Motherly. "It will all be okay," she said. "You'll see."

I gave her a small smile in return, and hoped she was right.

****

After spending the rest of my afternoon shopping, and mulling over Dr. Hansen's advice, I took a slow, leisurely drive to Huntley and Grayson's house. They were having a barbeque with the family to celebrate news of Huntley's pregnancy. I always looked forward to their barbeques and after an enlightening session with Dr. Hansen, I was excited to spend the evening enjoying myself with the people I cared about the most.

I came to a stop outside their house and grabbed Huntley's gift from the backseat. It was a spur of the moment purchase, something that would mean a lot to her, to both of us. I walked in without knocking, and followed the sound of loud chatter and laughter coming from outside on the deck. Huntley's face lit up when she saw me and made her way towards me, embracing me without hesitation. I hadn't seen her for two weeks while her and Grayson were on their honeymoon in Paris. I'd missed her fiercely.

"I'm so happy to see you," she said with a broad grin on her face. She was absolutely glowing.

"You too," I replied, returning her grin. "I missed you."

"I missed you too," she replied. I took her gift out and handed it to her.

"What is this?"

"Open it."

She lifted the lid off the small pink box and took out the necklace with the heart pendant. It was engraved with *'A best friend is a sister that Destiny forgot to give you"*.

"It's beautiful," she sniffled. She waved me off when I wanted to ask her what was wrong and said, "Hormones, don't mind me. I love it."

Just then, Grayson stepped up to her side, not noticing her brief bout of blubbering, and pulled me into a bear hug. I laughed, and while it sounded strange falling from my lips, it felt good.

"I'm glad you guys are back," I said. "Two weeks is way too long."

Grayson chuckled and looked Huntley with pure adoration. "I had a hard time keeping her there that long. Three days in and she wanted to come home because she missed Hunter."

Huntley responded with a playful slap, and replied,

"You're such an ass, Gray. You know you missed him too!"

He winked at her and gave her a chaste kiss. "Whatever you say, wife."

They were so in love it was nauseating. And sweet. They were proof that true love and happy ever after's didn't only exist in the romance novels that crowded my e-reader.

I cleared my throat and a rose colored blush crept over Huntley's cheeks. "I'm going to say hi to everyone else. Try not to rip each other's clothes off while I'm gone."

"No promises," Grayson called out from behind me and again, I laughed. I made my way around the deck and said hello to Grayson's parents, noticing that Jeff had been absent. We hadn't spoken since the wedding and I missed him, but I understood his need for space. I just hoped we could, at some point, go back to being friends. I moved on to Huntley's aunt and uncle and then finally on to Brody's grandparents. I was talking to Brody's grandmother when i felt eyes burning into the back of my head. The fine hairs on the back of my neck stood at attention, and my skin prickled with awareness. I knew it was Brody before I turned around, but when our eyes met, my heart stuttered. He'd always had that effect on me. Everyone else disappeared and just like it had been before, it was just the two of us. His hair was a sexy disheveled mess and he looked incredible in his dark jeans and grey t-shirt. I caught the smirk that played on his lips and realized that I'd been ogling him. It couldn't be helped. It came naturally to me, despite all that had happened between us, and that familiar energy still pulsated between us. We had so much to talk about, and I wanted to talk to him, but only one thing mattered then.

He was home.

chapter twenty-two

BRODY

I stopped outside my grandparent's farmhouse and gave myself a moment a breath for the first time in two months. It had taken me that long to get my things packed up in Chicago and finish up my last month at Johnson Waterman. Thankfully Sienna's father hadn't kicked up a fuss after I handed in my resignation, and to my surprise neither did Sienna.

I was glad to finally be out of Chicago and back where I belonged.

My grandfather, Clay was sitting on the front porch, pipe in hand. I hopped out of my truck, thankful that Grayson had been kind enough to leave it at the airport for me, and walked up the porch steps. My grandfather stood, and gave me the once over.

"It's about time you showed up, boy. Been waitin' for you for over a year."

I chuckled and gave him a hug. "I know, I know. Took me a little longer to figure my shit out," I replied.

"Well," he said, patting me on the back, "none of that matters. You're home now."

The font screen door opened and my grandmother, Luanne appeared, her mouth wrinkling at the side from her wide smile.

"Hi grandma."

She wordlessly wrapped her thin arms around my waist and squeezed. I kissed her gray hair and relaxed, breathing in her sweet familiar scent. I barely remembered my parents but as far as I was concerned, I didn't need them if I had people like Clay and Luanne Scott taking care of me.

"Welcome home, Brody. We're so happy you're back for good."

"Me too," I said into her hair.

She pulled away and looked up at my face. "We've missed you."

I wiped a stray tear from her aged cheek and tried to squelch the guilt I felt. Demi wasn't the only I'd inadvertently left behind.

"I'm home now," I told her, "and I have no intention of ever leaving again."

My grandmother cupped my cheek. "That makes me so happy to hear."

My grandfather cleared his throat. "Enough now, Luanne. Boy's been home all of five minutes and you're already smothering him."

"Oh hush," she slapped him on the chest, "I was not." She looked back up at me, laughter in her eyes. "I just made some fresh sweet tea. Why don't you sit outside here with your granddaddy and I'll bring you some."

"Sounds good, thank you Gama."

She disappeared inside and my grandfather resumed his

seat while I took the chair next to him. We were quiet for a while, almost contemplative as we both stared out onto the open land in front of us. My grandmother brought us some sweet tea as promised and shared a look with my grandfather before disappearing inside.

"You know," he began, "I was just a few years younger than you are now when I married your grandmother." His face transformed from the hard look I had always known growing up and softened. He let out a low whistle, and I listened while he spoke. "Man oh man, she was the prettiest young thing I'd ever seen, and we were so smitten people starting getting sick of it. Anyway, our parents were so mad when we decided to get hitched, but we didn't care. Your grandmother was it for me and we didn't see any point in waiting. It was a few years later when things got tough and we reached a point in our marriage where we weren't sure if we could make it work. We decided some time apart would be best, and I honestly thought it was over."

"I didn't know that," I said. "Why are you telling me now?"

"Because it damn near tore us apart," he replied. "And you know what I realized?"

I shook my head, not sure where he as going with this.

"I realized that I could live without your grandmother, but I just didn't want to."

"I still don't know why you're telling me this, Gramps."

"Why did you come home, son?" he asked, suddenly switching gears.

"Because I was unhappy in Chicago," I replied, perplexed.

"We both know it's more than that."

He stared at me and I finally understood why we were having this conversation.

"You came back for Demi," he stated, very sure of himself. My first instinct was to deny it, so I did.

"That's not true, Gramps. Demi and I are over. But you know all this."

"I know you don't believe that."

"Why else would I have come home?"

"You realized that you could live with out her, but you are choosing not to."

I looked at my grandfather, the man who had raised me taught me about what it took to be a man.

"Have you spoken to her yet?" he asked.

I put my elbows on my knees and pulled my fingers through my hair, the weight of the last two months resting heavily on my shoulders.

"No," I replied. "I'm not sure I'm ready for that yet."

"Bullshit," he said loudly. I was taken by surprise. He never cursed. "You came back to fight for her, didn't you?"

I couldn't lie to this man, but I wasn't sure. Had I come back to fight for Demi? I didn't even know if there was anything still worth fighting for.

Before I could say as much, my grandmother came outside.

"It's almost time to get leave for Huntley and Grayson's barbeque. You boys nearly ready?"

"I'm ready," my grandfather replied, "I don't need all day to get ready like you women do." He was teasing, and like most times, he was doing it to get a rise out of my grandmother.

She pointed her index in his direction and fixed him with her stern yet exuberant gaze. "Don't sass me Clayton Scott." He stood up and walked towards her, encasing her in his arms. "I wouldn't dream of it, sweetheart." He pressed a kiss to her lips, and I looked away to give them some privacy. Not to mention it was weird as hell watching your grandparents make out like teenagers. In many ways, I envied them. Who would've thought? They had the kind of love people write novels about, and I wasn't too much of a man to admit that I wanted it.

"Are you coming with us?" my grandmother asked after they'd unlocked their lips.

"I'll join you a little later," I replied. "I'm going to take a shower and unpack first."

"Don't take too long," my grandfather said. "I'm sure Grayson is eager to see you and catch up."

"Yes sir." I gave them a half smile and grabbed my bags from my truck. As soon as my grandparents had left, I hopped in the shower and got ready. I wasn't even sure I'd be seeing Demi tonight, but I couldn't ignore the small part of me that was hoping I would.

****

Grayson greeted me at the front door, followed by a rather enthusiastic Hunter.

"Good to have you home," Grayson said.

"I could say the same thing. You guys have a good honeymoon?"

His face broke into a grin and he replied, "Yeah, we had fun." He winked and I pretended to slug him in the arm.

"T.M.I man, really. I don't need to know that shit."

Grayson laughed as we made our way outside, but stopped just before we reached the door. He hesitated, and then looked back at me. "Demi's here," he said carefully, no doubt waiting for my reaction.

"I was counting on it."

He gave me a *its about fucking time* smile and I followed him outside. I wasn't sure what I was going to say to Demi when I saw her, but I'd figured it would come to me as soon as she was in front of me.

Huntley appeared in front of me, a knowing smile on her face. Did everyone know why I'd really come home except for me?

"Welcome home," she said with a hug. "It's about damn time."

"Nice to see you too, Mrs. Carter."

She beamed and damn if I wasn't happy for them.

"She's over there," Huntley pointed behind her, "talking to your grandparents."

"Thanks" I replied. "You think she'll talk to me?"

Huntley looked back at Demi and then at me. "I think you have to try. We're all rooting for you." Her eyes softened and she touched my arm. "Don't let me down."

I dipped my head and made my way towards Demi just as she turned her head. Our eyes clashed, green to brown, and I was instantly thrown back in high school. My hands started sweating, and I rubbed them on my jeans. It didn't help. My heart raced, blood rushing to my ears. Dammit, I was nervous.

"Hi," I said, stepping up to her. My grandparents sidled away quietly, leaving me alone with Demi.

"Hey," she replied quietly. Her light, faded jeans clung to her body, making it obvious that she's lost weight. Her black blouse hung loosely around her middle, but still managed to show off the curves I'd fallen in love with. Her eyes were a little dull, and her face a little more hollow than the last time I'd seen her. She looked gaunt, but still gorgeous. She'd always be gorgeous in my eyes.

"Uh…" I stuttered. Fucking nerves. "Can we go somewhere and talk?"

She looked apprehensive, somewhat hesitant. "I don't think now's the time or the place."

"Please," I persisted. "It won't take long."

"Okay," she sighed. I followed her through Huntley and Grayson's house and out the front door to the driveway. It was a strange place to have this conversation, but I guess it was as good as any. It was the only place we could get some privacy.

She stopped next to Huntley's grey jeep and turned to face me. We stared at each other, as if to relearn what the other looks like. On the outside we might've looked the same, but inside we'd changed. For better or worse only time would tell.

I swallowed, and took a leap. "We have a lot to talk about and - "

"I'm sorry," she blurted. "For all of it."

I relaxed slightly, thinking that 'sorry' was a good place to start. "So am I. We made a real mess of things."

"I should told you about..." she blinked, hesitating, "the baby. I was wrong to keep it from you."

"You're right," I admitted. "You should've. But if I hadn't have left, then maybe things would have been different."

"It wasn't your fault, and it wasn't mine. We made some stupid decisions, reckless decisions."

I rubbed my face. "I know."

"Do you think we can move on?" Her eyes shone bright with hope, a hope that mirrored mine.

"Things can never be the same, you know that."

Her face fell and she looked down. "I understand." Her voice was quiet, and broken. "Well, maybe we can be friends again, somewhere in the near future. Despite everything, I still want you to be happy Brody."

What just happened? Clearly she'd misunderstood what I meant. I grabbed her arm as she turned around, and stopped her.

"I don't think you understand what I'm saying."

She frowned, a line forming between her brows. The instinct to smooth it over with my thumb, like I always had, was overwhelming.

"I think I do," she replied. "You want us to move on."

"I do. Together."

We stood in silence and I took the chance to continue. I

thought about giving her a fancy, romantic speech, but she deserved more. She deserved the truth. I stepped closer and she tipped her head back.

"I know we have a lot to work through, but it all comes down to one thing," I paused, trying to steady the thump of my heart, "I miss you. I miss waking up with you next to me. I miss seeing you walk around barefoot in the kitchen. I miss kissing you," I brushed her bottom lip with my thumb, smiling when she sucked in a breath, "I miss hearing you sing in the shower. I miss making love to you at all hours. I miss having angry sex with you. I miss having you in my life, Demetria, and I know I can live without you, but dammit, I don't want to."

"I've missed you too," she choked out, "but how do we move on from everything? After everything we've put each other through?"

I cupped the back of her head and inched my face closer to hers. "It won't be easy," I replied in a whisper, "but if you're willing, I figured we could just…begin again."

Demi's eyes glistened in the moonlight and I wanted so much to erase the last year. But I couldn't. All I could do was express my willingness to fight, and hope to God she'd do the same.

"Fight for us," I breathed. "Decide that everything we've been through isn't enough to stop you from fighting for us."

I could tell by the way her eyes searched mine that she was contemplating it. I started getting nervous again. At least it wasn't a flat out no.

"What about Sienna?" She flinched. "She's pregnant."

I shook my head. I was planning on explaining this all to her later, but now I had no other choice.

"She lied. She was never pregnant."

"Oh."

I waited, and then asked, "What are you thinking?"

"I'm thinking...that I really want you to kiss me right now."

I took my chance and crashed my lips to hers. Our mouths moved with familiarity, certainty. I knew her mouth, her lips, their taste, and yet my body was hot all over like it was our first kiss. Her tongue ventured into my mouth and she coaxed mine into a wicked dance of give and take. Her hands fisted in my shirt, and mine slid into her hair, pulling her head back so that I could deepen the kiss. I swallowed her moan just as she swallowed mine. It was perfect.

Until we heard cheering and clapping coming from what I knew to be living room of Huntley and Grayson's house. Demi and I broke apart, both breathless and desperate for air. We looked to the side and found our closest friends and family watching us. They all smiled like idiots and cheered us on.

"Oh God," Demi muttered into my chest. "How embarrassing."

I chuckled. "At least they got a show, but you never gave *me* an answer."

"Can we take it slow?" she asked.

I brushed her lips with mine, feeling the way her body shivered from the contact. "We can take it as slow as you want."

"Sounds perfect."

chapter twenty-three

3 Months Later

DEMI

Fingers trailed down my spine and cupped my butt cheek. My skin broke out into goose flesh and I felt my nipples harden.

"Hmm." Brody hummed next to my ear as his hand dipped between my legs. I squirmed, earning a chuckle from the beautiful man next to me. The rich timber of his voice made heat pool between my legs. I wanted him. Again. And judging by the erection pressing into my side, he was thinking the same thing.

"Good morning," I murmured. I turned my head to face him and he gave me that panty dropping *I'm going to make you scream my name* smile. His brown eyes lured me in, like they always had, and in them I saw everything I'd always wanted.

"It will be very soon," he replied. I saw the gleam in his eye and my insides coiled in delicious anticipation. He was insatiable, had been since last night. It was the first time we'd had sex since he'd come home and while it was torture to wait, I was glad he'd made good on his promise to take it slow. We'd worked through the things we needed to, taken one day at a time, and the result was not a mended relationship, but a completely new one. Brody made me believe he wanted me and he showed me every day that we were meant to be.

Last night, Brody had taken me on a date, something we'd never done before. He did all the things a woman would expect on a date - bought me flowers, opened the door for me, took me to a nice restaurant, made me laugh - and when we finally got home I couldn't take it anymore. I dragged him back to my bedroom and we spent the rest of the night learning each other's bodies from scratch.

I turned over and before I could blink he had me beneath him. The hard planes of his chest pressed down on my breasts and he settled between my legs, his erection hot against my belly. My blood simmered beneath my skin.

"There she is," he said, his full lips stretched into a grin. "I was worried you weren't going to wake up at all."

I pushed my hands through his hair and cradled his head. "It's not my fault you tired me out," I sighed lazily. "I'm worried you might've broken me."

He smirked, and if I wasn't already wet I was now. "We'll have to find out now won't we?"

My heart started beating double time and my skin prickled with awareness. He pulled a pebbled nipple into his mouth and bit down before licking away the sharp sting. The intensity could be felt all the way down below where his hips rested on mine.

"I love these," he murmured, palming my other breast. I arched my back but we never broke eye contact. Something about it made it even more sensual. His hand slid further down, his fingers feather light, until they brushed my tender lips. I bit my lip and whimpered.

"This," Brody whispered, "Is.Mine." He pushed two fingers into me and rubbed my clit with his thumb.

"Brody," I sighed, "Hmmmm."

I felt the tension start low and build, hoping for that inevitable release. Then Brody stopped, and I had to stop myself from scowling.

"Don't worry, Demetria," the way he said my name made me shiver, "I have…bigger…plans for you."

My eyes broke from his, only to land on where he'd positioned the head of his cock at my opening. He pushed in, slowly, gently, and it was the most violent pleasure to feel him fill me up. He braced himself on his forearms and threaded his fingers through my hair. My hands trailed down his back and dipped into the deep crevices formed by his muscles.

"I love you," I whispered against his mouth, "so much."

"I love you too," he replied. He devoured my mouth, feasting on me like he was a starved man. His hips started moving, slowly at first, and then faster and harder. I wrapped my legs around him and hitched my knees up under his arms. The slight change in my position took him deeper and the tip of his cock hit my sweet spot.

We grew sweaty, clinging to each other for dear life, and when his eyes met mine I was sure nothing could ever break us up again.

I sucked in a breath and mouth formed an "o" as my impending orgasm took over my entire body.

"So beautiful." Brody's voice sounded far away. My body shook, and my eyes rolled backward. Brody hovered above me and then bit my neck as he found is own release. We were a mess of sweaty limbs, damp skin and heavy breathing. It was the perfect mess to be in.

Brody finally came up for air and stared down at my flushed face.

"Make me a promise," I said, still trying to catch my breath.

"Anything," he replied without hesitating. My insides warmed knowing he would do anything for me without question. God, I really did love him.

"Promise me you'll never leave me again."

He brushed his thumb across my cheek and I saw the regret in the depths of his chocolate orbs. It took me back to the night we cried together over the loss of the child we would never get to meet. I kept a box of all my sonograms, and the tiny pink booties that once belonged to me as a baby. I'd kept them in the hopes that I was having a little girl. It was hard, going through all those things with Brody, but in many ways grieving together, even after so much time had passed, healed us and allowed us to move on. Together.

"I promise. I'm not going anywhere ever again. My heart is yours, and I don't want to be anywhere you're not."

I swore I was done crying but his words, his promise, reached into me and touched my soul. We were bound together for life and I realized that I wouldn't have done anything differently. All the bad stuff, all the heartache had led us right back to where we were meant to be. And all because we decided to *begin again…*

epilogue

2 Years Later

DEMI

The sun had set and in its place was a beautiful night sky littered with millions of stars. The sound of crickets echoed around us. Brody covered my eyes and spoke into my ear. "No peaking." He led me away from our newly built house.

I giggled. "Where are you taking me?" I almost tripped but his arm wrapped around my waist to steady me. He chuckled, most likely at my clumsiness.

"It's a surprise," he whispered, "just trust me."

I thought about where he could be taking me, since there were few places on the ranch I didn't know, but I knew it was pointless. If he said it was a surprise, I believed him.

We'd moved onto the ranch a few months ago and already I felt at home. Brody was finally chasing his dreams, only this time with me at his side. Between Grayson, Brody and Jeff, they had managed to start a flourishing business and had plans to later expand. I was happy for them and shared in their excitement.

I heard a door creak open and there only one place we could possibly be. The barn.

Brody ushered me in and we came to a stop. "Stay right here," he told me, "I'm going to remove my hand but you have to keep those pretty eyes closed. Understood?"

I nodded, growing antsy. "Okay."

His hand left my face and I heard him walk away. There were a few hushed voices around me, and I frowned. What the hell was going on?

Less then a minute later, Brody took my hands in his and pulled me in a little further.

"Open your eyes, Demetria."

My lids opened and an audible gasp left my mouth. All our closest friends and family were gathered around us in a wide circle and the barn was lit up by hundreds of tea lights. I looked up, and it was almost like looking at stars.

I looked back at Brody, confused.

"What's going on?" I asked.

He smiled that shy smile I loved so much and it dawned on me that he was anxious. He never got anxious. Something weird was happening.

"You were five when we met," he started, squeezing my hands, "and that first day I told you your dress was ugly. Your answer was to throw a mudpie in my face." People laughed, and then everything went quiet again. You could hear a pin drop.

Brody swallowed and then continued, "I knew then that there was no one else out there for me. Only you." Oh. Shit. I knew what was coming. "Demetria Rosemead, I have loved you all my life. I believe after all of the hardships we've faced, we ended up right here, right now, in front of all our friends and family so that I could tell you how much I love you. I love that sassy mouth, " I laughed, feeling the tears coming, "I love that smart mind. I love every curve on your body," someone cleared a throat and I blushed furiously, "I love the way you make me feel, and the way you've given yourself to me so completely. I love that every day is a new adventure, and the way you always make me laugh. I love the confidence you exude and how you care for our friends. But most of all, I love your heart."

He bent down on one knee and I cupped my mouth. This was really happening. He pulled out a blue box and in it sat a beautiful platinum band with a princess cut diamond. It was ornate, and it sparkled as it caught the shimmering of the tea lights above us.

"Two years ago, almost to the day, I made you a promise to never leave your side, and now it's my turn to ask you for that same promise. Marry me."

I bent down and cupped his face. "Yes, Brody Scott, I will marry you."

His face broke out into a brilliant smile and the people around us cheered loudly. We both stood up, and slipped the ring onto my finger before smashing his mouth to mine. Everyone else disappeared and it was just the two of us. As I kissed him, my *fiancé,* I finally had everything I'd ever wanted. I'd lost it all, only to gain something much better and much bigger than I could have imagined.

about the author

Tamsyn is a 22 year old blogger turned author who has an insatiable hunger for New Adult Contemporary Romance novels, coffee and chocolate. When she's not getting caught up in yet another steamy romance with a new book boyfriend, she can be found spending endless hours working away on her laptop in pursuit of her Marketing degree and a career in book Publishing. Tamsyn is a brat when it comes to books and believes that every story, no matter how challenging, should have a Happy Ever After.

Social Media/Stalker Links:

Facebook:
www.facebook.com/pages/Tamsyn-Bester/635202666493424
Goodreads:
www.goodreads.com/author/show/6965463
Twitter:
@TamsynBester

also by tamsyn

BENEATH YOUR BEAUTIFUL

On the outside, Huntley Morgan is your typical girl-next-door, with her long blonde hair and piercing blue eyes, and that's exactly what she wants people to see. Her name exposes her to the demons of her past but remembering her reason for moving across the country to start over is what keeps her alive. For the first time since the brutal murder of her mother, Huntley allows herself to care about the people around her.

Grayson Carter has everything a 21yr old College Senior could wish for - he's the star of Whitley University's football team, he has a different girl willing to be in his bed every night and a supportive family. For years he has managed keep his family together and hide their dark secrets from the small town of Breckinridge, Alabama.

When Huntley and Grayson meet, a force so strong pulls them together in a hurricane of feelings neither of them could have ever anticipated. Huntley and Grayson try to stay away from each other, but when Huntley's demons seek her out, their pasts become the biggest storm of all.

Will they learn to trust each other and build a new future together or will they simply do nothing to prevent history from repeating itself?

DESTINED TO FALL

When Cassey Emerson graduated high school 3 years ago, she packed her bags and left the dusty trailer park she called home in the rear view mirror. Since then, she has worked hard to give herself the life, and career, that she always dreamed of. As the Publishing Assistant at Knight Media, her dreams are slowly but surely coming true…

But something is missing…

Kyler Knight is young, rich and the heir to the multi-million dollar fortune that is known as 'Knight Media' – the biggest and most successful media company in Chicago. When his father decides it's time for Kyler to learn the ropes as successor, he didn't think it would include working with someone like Cassey Emerson.

Their attraction is immediate and Kyler is everything Cassey should stay away from. He can't give her what she wants, but that doesn't stop him from pursuing her. When one passionate night changes everything, Cassey must decide whether or not she can accept what Kyler is offering, or walk away from how he makes her feel.

Suddenly, things change, lines are blurred, hearts are broken and Cassey is left to pick up the pieces after her hot, steamy relationship with Kyler becomes so much more…

Can she move forward or was she always *destined to fall*?

PRECIOUS CONSEQUENCES

All it took was one night to change the rest of my life.

One night that created irrevocable consequences.

But some consequences aren't all bad.

They can be amazing...beautiful... ***Precious***.

I willingly accepted those consequences and wrote a new plan for my life. But that plan didn't include Cameron Argent - the sexy-as-sin tattooed playboy who got under my skin the moment I laid eyes on him. I was headed down a dark and dangerous road where he was concerned and in the end, our relationship was inevitable. Despite our dark secrets, our feelings for each other burned brighter than a thousand stars and left us both naked, vulnerable.

But when my past came rolling back into my life like a Summer storm, I wasn't sure if his love for me was enough.

Was he prepared to deal with the consequences of a past I couldn't regret or would he walk away with my beating heart in his hands?

playlist

All Of Me – **John Legend**

Begin Again – **Taylor Swift**

Broken – **Lifehouse**

Cowboy Take Me Away – **Dixie Chicks**

Fade Into You – **Sam Palladio & Claire Bowen**

How Long Will I Love You – **Ellie Goulding**

Maybe Someday – **Griffin Peterson**

Nothing In This World – **Hayden Panettiere**

Not Ready To Make Nice – **Dixie Chicks**

Say Something – **A Great Big World**

Stubborn – **The Lumineers**

Whiskey – **Jana Kramer**

Why Ya Wanna – **Jana Kramer**

Wrecking Ball – **Miley Cyrus**

You And Me – **Lifehouse**

Printed in Great Britain
by Amazon.co.uk, Ltd.,
Marston Gate.